This book has been donated to
school children within Muskegon County
through the generosity of our community.

Distributed through

MAISD

Muskegon Area
Intermediate School District

Pitcher's Hands is OUT!

Dan Bylsma
&
Jay M. Bylsma

River Road Publications, Inc.

Spring Lake, Michigan

Hardcover ISBN: 0-938682-65-2
Paperback ISBN: 0-938682-66-0
Printed in the United States of America

Contents

Special Thanks

Writing a book about a time period one didn't experience requires a lot of resources. We were fortunate to have people who gave generously of their memories and experiences and their memorabilia without which, this endeavor would have been much more difficult and in some cases, not possible.

The following individuals deserve our appreciation and special mention:

Lynne Deur who had the idea for *Pitcher's Hands is OUT!* in the first place and whose only shortcoming may have been to choose us to write it.

John Oole (d.), our father-in-law and grandfather who couldn't pull peppermints out of kid's ears but had them in his pockets and who worked in the banks at the time of the Bank Holidays.

Ralph Secory (d.) because no historical novel of baseball in "Grand Harbor" would be authentic if the name Secory were left out.

Lois Nagtzaam, Clarence "Tad" Poel, Curtis Jones, and Jerry Banninga - a wonderful lady and three great gentlemen who lived the Depression and who shared their fascinating personal stories with us. Unfortunately, while they will recognize some of their tales, many of them could only give the book a flavoring.

Don Nagtzaam who actually played Boy Scout baseball for Troop 23 in "Grand Harbor" in 1936 and did drive his uncle's fishing tug at age 10.

Robert E. Witham who shared his photographs and recollection of the 1936 Packard automobile.

Carl "Bub" Denton for sharing his name, his 1936 Boy Scout manual, and his Boy Scout Troop number.

Theodore S. VanderVeen, M.D. for patching up both of us from our bumps on the noggin over the years and his medical advice about concussions.

The Card Collectors Company for furnishing the T206 set of baseball cards.

Mike Payne's book "300 Great Baseball Cards" for some valuable information in a world in which we are rank amateurs.

A girl one of us remembers only as "Mitzie" and Mary Beth Friel (now Bylsma)who taught us that girls could be as good in athletics as boys if given a chance.

Tom Hammond and Ben Stone who allowed us to incorporate their real baseball stories into our fictional one. They really did what their namesakes do in our story.

Chaim Potok, Pulitzer prize winning novelist (a real writer) from whose wonderful first book, *The Chosen* we borrowed a well known incident.

William Brashler from whose book *Josh Gibson, A Life in the Negro Leagues* we drew invaluable information.

David H. Seibold, D.D.S. whose book *Coast Guard City, USA - A History of the Port of Grand Haven* was a great source of information about the history of "Grand Harbor."

Miss Nettie Abrams, Jay's eighth grade teacher - a wonderful, dignified and gracious Jewish lady who taught in a Christian school.

To these and also to those whose names, nicknames, or personas we used: Gertude "widow" Baak (d)., Harley "Beans" Mulder (d.), Abraham "Brum" Nagtzaam (d.), Percival Van Doorne (d.), Bob Kleinhecksel, Mike Beck, David Berilla, and Kasey "Cassandra Lynnea" Bylsma, our thanks.

To the Reader

Pitcher's Hands Is OUT! is set in a time period called the Great Depression, which started in America in 1929 and continued to the beginning of World War II in 1941. During this time millions of Americans lost their jobs and often their homes when they were unable to pay their mortgages or rent. Twice people in Michigan (where the story takes place) experienced a bank holiday, meaning all banks had to close and people could not take out their money. When the banks were allowed to reopen, some of them couldn't. They were insolvent because their deposits (what they owed their customers) were greater than the money they were able to collect from the people and businesses they had made loans to.

Under President Franklin D. Roosevelt the government set up programs that gave people jobs and at least some money to help them survive. One was the Works Progress Administration, or the WPA, which created jobs ranging from teaching to building hospitals or libraries. Another was the Civilian Conservation Corps, ofr CCC, which gave jobs to young men. The men lived in various camps across the country and built roads and parks, planted treees or fought forest fires. Most of the money they earned was sent home to their families.

Overall, the Great Depression was a frightening time for everyone, including Scooter Secory and his family, the characters in this novel. They didn't know that the difficult financial times would end. Unfortunately, they ended with an even more frightening event. What people called The Great War would look minor compared to what was to happen. America became involved in the biggest war the world had ever known—World War II.

Chapter 1

Scooter

The scariest thing in Gregory Peter Secory's life so far was that his family had to move to a different town to live with his grandfather. Bogeymen under the bed at night after the lights went out were nothing compared to leaving all your friends, your school, and your neighborhood to move to a new city. But it was 1936 and difficult economic times were being felt by lots of folks.

The first hint of tragedy for Gregory's family came when the governor of Michigan declared a bank holiday, meaning all the banks had to close. About the only good thing about the bank holiday was that there weren't any bank robberies for eight days. The bad thing was that people couldn't get their own money out of the bank so they had to rob piggy banks for money to buy gas and groceries. When the banks began to reopen, some of the banks didn't or couldn't. They owed their customers more money than they could collect from the people and businesses they had loaned money to.

Shortly after that President Franklin Roosevelt

declared another bank holiday. This time when the banks began to reopen, the Grand Rapids First Trust Bank, where Gregory's father Peter Secory had his life savings, did not reopen.

The Secorys had $462 dollars in their savings account at the First Trust Bank. It was enough to buy a new car or go a long way toward buying a modest house. But it was gone, and there wasn't anything the Secorys could do about it. From then on the bank would be bitterly remembered as the False Trust Bank

Then three years later, without much warning, the Royal Machine Shop where Gregory's father worked as a machinist went out of business. They made parts for diesel engines. But in hard times the demand for diesel engine parts had dried up and Mr. Secory lost his job. Day after day he would leave the house full of hope and confidence that he would find a new job. But day after day he would come home with only hope, hope that he might find a job the next day—or the next.

First the Secory family had to give up their car. It was only the second time Gregory saw his father cry—the first was when his mother, Gregory's grandmother, died. The car was not only Mr. Secory's pride and joy, but now he would have to walk or take the streetcar to continue his job hunting. It would make the task of finding a job more difficult.

As the weeks and months went by and there was still no job, Gregory could hear his mom and dad talking in hushed tones long after he went to bed at night. His mother's eyes were often red and swollen. Gregory suspected it came from crying, but he never actually saw her tears. Easter came and went. There were no Easter baskets with colored eggs and chocolate bunnies or a new Sunday shirt and tie for either Gregory or his younger brother, Russell.

"I'll make it up to you next year, sweetie. I promise," his mother had said with a catch in her voice.

Until now Gregory's family actually had been luckier than some because his dad had kept his job for several years after the Great Depression started with the Stock Market Crash of 1929. There were kids in his class whose fathers had lost their jobs right away and now worked on government projects building roads and bridges for the government for 33 cents an hour. It was a program started by President Roosevelt called WPA. Its real name was the Work Projects Administration, but people with real jobs said that WPA stood for We Putter Around.

Unfortunately for Peter Secory, the WPA projects

in Western Michigan were winding down in 1936. There was no need for additional workers even in this program, which was supposed to create jobs for folks who couldn't find work.

Now the Secorys, like many other families, had to muddle through on their own or with the help of their neighbors or their church. Many's the day when a neighbor would bring their leftovers or a small casserole to the Secory's where it was gratefully accepted.

As spring brought out the tulips, it also brought out the baseball bats and mitts. The lot across Century Avenue came alive with the shouts of sandlot baseball games. They were called sandlot games because any vacant lot big enough to play baseball on would soon have its weeds trampled down to the dirt or sand. And there was enough room between Century Avenue and the railroad tracks for a ball field. It was at this field that Gregory Peter Secory had first been introduced to baseball.

The game had mesmerized him when he first saw the older boys of the neighborhood play their endless games of work-up. These were not games with two teams of nine players and umpires and all that. There were only seven or eight kids who would play. The first batter was decided by a game of "Ibbidy Bibbidy" or by a chorus of "first-ups" where the kid who shouted "first-up" first and or loudest (or was the biggest or meanest) got to bat first. The first player to shout "pitcher" would pitch.

Two batters would begin the game with the other players taking positions in the field. Batters would bat until they were put out. Then they would go to the outfield and the pitcher would become a batter. The first baseman would then become pitcher and so on. The players in the field would work their way up to bat by getting batters out, which is how the game got its name of "work-up."

Because it was impossible to have enough players to cover all the bases with only five or six fielders, it was customary to call "pitcher's hands is out." This rule meant that if a ground ball was thrown to the pitcher before the batter reached first base, the batter was out. "Automatic second" was a rule by which a batter who safely reached first base could leave first base and go to second before the next batter batted without being put out if there were only enough players to have two batters.

At first Gregory was too small to play. Besides, he had no mitt to play with or bat or ball to contribute to the game. But he made himself useful by going behind the batter, retrieving balls and tossing those balls back to the pitcher. Because he wanted to be part of the game and to be thought of as useful, Gregory would hustle after every pitch that passed the batter.

"What's your name, kid?" one of the players asked him after a few games of being the all-time catcher.

"Gregory Secory."

"What kind of name is Secory?" It was a loaded question and Gregory knew it. The southwest side of Grand Rapids, Michigan, was largely made up of people whose parents or grandparents came from the Netherlands. There weren't any people of Italian or Polish descent in his neighborhood. They mostly lived on the northwest side of the city.

The divisions in Grand Rapids were largely religious. Protestants lived on the southwest side. Catholics were on the Northwest side. These were tight-knit communities. They worshipped together, went to school together, played together, worked together, and shopped with their own shopkeepers. Folks from the other neighborhoods were commonly referred to with ethnic names, like Mackerel Snappers or Wops and Polacks. They were tolerated best from a distance.

Young Gregory only shrugged his shoulders.

Actually, he didn't know what kind of a name Secory was. It could be short for Vander Secory, which would have been acceptable in this neighborhood. Or it could be short for Secorski or Secorinelli, which would have been near fatal.

"Well, never no mind. You can be all-time catcher if you scoot after the balls and be quick about it. You can be our scooter."

And with those words Gregory Peter Secory became Scooter. Not someone who was called Scooter, he became Scooter. Oh, in school and in catechism classes at church the teachers addressed him as Gregory Secory and when his parents were angry with him, he was Gregory Peter Secory. But in his boyhood world he was Scooter. And like most good nicknames, it defined him a way. He somehow looked like what a Scooter would look like. He was small for his age and he was fast. When he played his beloved baseball, he played with a lot of hustle and drive.

Being called Scooter didn't bother Gregory. It was, after all, his ticket to be all-time catcher when the older boys played work-up. Then he came to realize that there were a lot of major league baseball players with nicknames. There was Babe whose real name was George Herman Ruth, for example, and Dizzy whose name was Jay Dean, and Goose whose real name was Leon Goslin. There was even a guy who was called Pie Traynor who played for the Pittsburgh Pirates. And it was a lot better to be called Scooter than Babe or Dizzy or Goose or, heaven forbid, Pie!

Now that he was older, Gregory Secory was no longer all-time catcher, but he was still Scooter. He was there when first-ups was called and he played until he was called in for supper or it was too dark to see the ball. He was as good as any player on the lot, except for one problem. He didn't have a baseball mitt. His parents simply had no money for a baseball mitt. But Scooter did have something almost as important–he had a bat.

Just before the Royal Machine Shop had closed, Scooter and his father found a fallen branch from an ash tree. Using a hand saw, his father had cut the branch to about the length of a bat. Then he took it to the machine shop where he worked. Scooter was fascinated as his father put the branch into a machine called a lathe. He mounted the branch horizontally between two holder-like things. The branch looked like his mother's rolling pin.

On an overhead shaft a large leather belt looped around a big wheel or pulley and connected to a small pulley on the lathe. The shaft turned very fast and made a lot of noise. When his father pulled a lever, the machine caused the wood to spin rapidly. Then his father took a sharp tool and carefully moved the tool up and down the whirling branch. First the bark came curling off the branch. As his father applied more pressure against the branch, the tool peeled off more wood.

Several times his father changed tools and skillfully applied them to the spinning wood. As he worked, a bat began to take shape before Scooter's astonished eyes. When it looked finished, Mr. Secory took a strip of sandpaper and looped it around the spinning bat. The contact of the sandpaper with the spinning bat made its surface as smooth as the legs of their dining room table. It was the most beautiful bat Scooter had ever seen.

Mr. Secory removed the bat from the lathe and took it to a workbench. "How 'bout if I burn your name in it so's everyone will know just whose bat this is?"

Scooter nodded his approval.

"Lemme see, what would you like? Just your first name or your whole name?"

Scooter hesitated. In this new bat's world, he wasn't Greg or Gregory or Gregory Secory, or Gregory Peter Secory. He was Scooter. "I'd like you to burn 'Scooter.'"

"Scooter? Where'd that come from?"

"It's what my friends call me. Some kids in the neighborhood don't even know my real name."

His father looked at him thoughtfully. "So you're Scooter now, are you? Then Scooter it'll be." He very carefully burned SCOOTER into the grain of the bat near the end away from the handle. "Just like a trademark," he said. "Remember to hold the trademark up when you bat, so's it doesn't break when you really get a hold of someone's fastball," he added as he handed the bat to Scooter.

Scooter hefted the bat. It had a sweet feel to it. He stepped back and swung the bat at an imaginary pitch.

"I think this bat's got some mighty big hits in it," his father said. "'Course, it'll be up to you to coax 'em out if it."

Wow! His very own bat—one that had been a tree branch only a few moments before. One that his father had crafted with his own hands. Wait until the sandlot guys got the feel of this, Scooter thought.

"Thanks, Dad. It's really neat!"

"You're welcome. Mind if I have a feel of her?"

Scooter handed the bat to his father, who gripped it with both hands and waggled it back and forth. "She's got good balance if I say so myself. Scooter, is it?" he said as he rubbed one hand over the name burned into the top of the bat. "I had a nickname when I was your age."

This revelation surprised Scooter. Somehow it was hard to believe that his father was ever as young as Scooter was now. He had seen pictures of his father taken when he was a boy, but the kid in the pictures seemed to be someone different than the tall man who now stood before him swinging a bat.

"What did kids call you?"

"T-Bone."

"T-Bone?" Scooter couldn't help but snicker. "Why'd they call you T-Bone?"

"I suppose because I was taller than most kids my age and had long arms. Once I stretched 'em out at my side, and someone thought I looked like a T-Bone."

"Did you like it, being called T-Bone I mean?"

"No, but there's worse nicknames. I didn't encourage it. It didn't last. I became Pete again before too long. Do you like Scooter?"

Scooter smiled and shrugged his shoulders,

"Kinda."

"Do you mind if I still call you Gregory?"

"No, sir."

"Scooter," Mr. Secory said. "Scooter. Sorta fits you, don't it?"

"Sorta."

"Well, Scooter, let's get these shavings cleaned up. Fetch the broom from the corner over there."

As it turned out, the bat had a bittersweet memory. It was made only a few days before the Royal Machine Shop closed and the Secory family began to feel the effects of the hard times that the newspapers called The Great Depression.

Now there was talk over the meager fare of dinner that if Mr. Secory didn't find a steady job soon, they would be unable to make the mortgage payments on their house. They might lose it just like they had lost the car. They would have to move. Different neighborhood, different school, different friends. That was scary enough, not to mention the worry that there might not be a place to play baseball—now that Gregory had a bat.

Chapter 2

Scooter's Grandpa

Scooter was awakened by a car horn tooting right below his bedroom window. The Saturday morning sun was already streaming around the corners of his window shades, reminding him there was no school today. He got out of bed and peered through the opening between the shade and the window frame. The sun was so bright his sleepy eyes had to squint to see anything at all. But he could see his Grandpa Secory getting out of his new 1936 Packard sedan, come from Grand Harbor for an unexpected visit. This was a great surprise. His grandfather always had a wide smile and a peppermint or two in his pocket, a treat Scooter hadn't had in awhile. And Scooter was anxious to show off his new bat, which he pulled from under his bed.

Scooter stored his favorite things under his bed. In case there was a fire they would be handy to find and save. He heard that one of his mother's brothers, Scooter's Uncle Fred, went to bed fully dressed with clean clothes so he wouldn't have to run out into the street in his pajamas in case there was a fire in the night. Uncle Fred was funny about other things, too. His mother said it was because he was "shell-shocked" during The Big War. He had seen some terrible things in the war and hadn't been "right in the head" since.

Even so, having your favorite things close at hand in case of a fire seemed like a good idea to Scooter. And under your bed was as close at hand as he could think of. He quickly pulled on his clothes, not even bothering to slip his suspender straps over his shoulders. Then he ran downstairs shouting, "Hey, everyone! Grampa Secory is here!"

In his haste to get to Grandpa Secory's car, Scooter forgot one of his father's rules and let the screen door slam shut. The "bam" of the screen door was followed almost immediately by his father's stern voice.

"Gregory Peter! How many times do I have to tell you about slamming the screen door? You march right back here and close the screen door properly. We've no money to be fixing foolishness!"

It seemed a little silly to go back and reclose a screen door that was already closed, but he had broken the rule and that was that. He hung his head in shame at his forgetfulness and came back, opened the screen door, went through it, and closed

it. Then he returned through it again, carefully clos-
ing the door as he should have in the first place.

"That's better. Don't forget it again!"

Both Scooter and his father turned their attention to the old gentleman who was coming around
the corner of the back of the house. He was labor-
ing, struggling to carry a loaded orange crate under each arm.

"Is there anyone around here who can help an
old man with a heavy load? I'm looking for a strong
young man," he said with a twinkle in his voice.

"Let me help you, Gramps," Scooter rose to the
challenge.

"I don't think so. These are heavy boxes. I think
I need someone a lot bigger and stronger than you.
I need a young man."

Then he raised his voice as if there were a large
crowd that he was speaking to. "Is there anyone
here big and strong enough to help an old man with
a heavy load? I've got money. I can pay for the right
help.

"Whoa. Whatdaya got there?" Grandfather had
spotted Scooter's bat.

"It's my new bat my father made it for me we
found a downed tree branch and he cut it to size
and made this bat for me on a machine at his shop

15

and I watched him and he burnt my name in it and everything. . ..." The words gushed out of Scooter's mouth so fast his Grandfather couldn't tell where the periods and the commas came.

"Whoa, Nellie. Slow down. I've got old ears that can't listen as fast as you can talk. Let me give one of these boxes to someone who's big and strong and then you can tell me again when I can hear faster. Where's your older brother anyway."

"I can take a box. I'm not Russell."

"What, you're not Russell? Well, who are you? Lord 'a mercy. Gregory! You grow so fast I didn't recognize you there for a minute. You been takin' growing pills or something? Last I saw you were knee-high to a grasshopper. Now look at you!"

"Grampa, you saw me just a few months ago. I haven't grown that much."

"Yes, well maybe it's because my eyes are just exactly as old as my ears, and I don't see so fast either. Here. You take one of these boxes and I'll tote the other.

"Hello Peter. Ruthie, my dear, you're as good-looking as the first day Peter brought you home. And there's my Russell. Landsakes but it's good to see you all." His patter didn't stop as he made his way through the back porch into the kitchen where he put his box down.

He gave Scooter's mother a hug and shook his son's hand. Then he turned his attention to Russell. "Russell, my boy, you look so much like your daddy looked when he was your age, I don't know whether I'm here and now or back there and then. How's my boy? I hear tell it's bad for your constitution to have sweets before noon, but it's noon somewheres. How about a peppermint? Let's see." The old gentleman began fumbling through his pockets. "I thought I put them here. No, not there. . .."

Scooter had seen his Grandfather's fumbling act a hundred times before, but he did it so well Scooter never knew for sure where the peppermints would show up. Even Russell knew the act and was starting to giggle.

"I'm sure I put a peppermint in my pocket before I left the house this morning." Grampa Secory was back searching in the same pockets he had fumbled through before. His pants, his shirt, his vest, back to his pants. Finally, apparently stumped as to where the peppermint was, he held out an empty hand, palm up, and pointed to it with his other. "No peppermint here," he said.

Then he swept his open hand around and pointed to the other hand which he opened to show it was also empty. "No peppermint here, either. Now where did the peppermint go?"

That was the family's cue to say, in unison, "I just don't knoooow."

Grandfather then put his hand under his chin with his forefinger pointing to his nose, as if he were thinking about a tough question. "I wonder where. . .. Oh, oh! I think I see it." He make a slow, dramatic gesture with his pondering hand to reach behind Russell's ear. "Ahh, it was there all along. You were hiding it behind your ear, you little rascal. Well, you'll have to get up earlier than you did this morning to fool your old Grampa!"

Once again, the old peppermint trick worked and Grampa Secory had pulled a peppermint out from behind someone's ear. Scooter had watched him do the trick dozens of times, but he still couldn't figure out how the old man did it.

He turned to Scooter. "So Gregory, I seem to be fresh out of peppermints. Are you hiding one behind your ear, too?" With that, the old man produced another peppermint, seemingly right out of Scooter's ear. "Gregory, you need to clean your ears better. I'll give you this peppermint, but remember it came out of your ear. I'm not sure how that will taste. How long has it been in there, do you suppose?"

"Aw, gee, Gramps. How'd you do that?" Scooter asked as he popped the peppermint into his mouth.

"Do what? Find a peppermint in your ear? These old eyes can't see fast, but even as slow as they are, they can still see a white peppermint the size of a quarter in someone's ear.

"Now let me see that new bat of yours, and why don't your hitch up those suspenders before your britches fall down and we catch sight of your drawers. You wearin' drop seats or split backs?"

"Grampa! I don't wear long johns in the summer time." Scooter giggled as he handed the bat to the old gentleman.

"Wow. Your papa made this for you?" the old man asked as he hefted the bat. "I was pricing these just the other day at the hardware store. Fella's asking six bits for a bat that wasn't this fine. Very nice work, Peter, very nice work indeed," he said as he admired the bat.

"Six bits. What is six bits?" Scooter had never heard the term before.

"A bit is twelve and a half cents. Two bits is a quarter, so six bits is seventy-fve cents," Scooter's father interjected.

"Scooter. Scooter? Who might that be?" Grandfather asked. He held the bat up almost to his eyes as if to see the trademark clearly while looking sideways at Gregory as if he hadn't figured out that Scooter was his grandson's nickname.

"That's what all the kids call me," Scooter replied as he hitched up his suspenders.

"What?" Scooter's mother was astonished. "Why, that's a terrible thing. Gregory is a perfectly good name. What's wrong with Gregory?"

"Gee willikers, Mom. Most kids have a nickname and Scooter's better than most."

"We don't set our standards by what most folks do. Most folks swear and chew and spit. Next thing that's what you'll be wanting to do, and I'll not have it."

"Didn't you have a nickname a time or two, Peter?" Grandfather asked Scooter's father, peering over his glasses at his son. "What was it? Redbone or sawbones? Something like that I seem to recollect."

"It was T-Bone," Scooter's father answered sheepishly, "and I didn't wear it for very long. I'm surprised you remember."

"T-Bone?" Mrs. Secory burst out laughing. "Peter, you never told me people used to call you T-Bone."

"That's because I'd almost forgotten, and if'n I'd a remembered, I wouldn't have told you because I knew you'd laugh."

"T-Bone. That's hilarious."

"So I suppose you never had a nickname?"

Scooter's mother laughed into a smile and she became quiet, as if she were remembering something nice. "My grandfather Schultz used to call me 'Snickelfritz.' He died when I was a little girl, and that's all I can remember about him. He had a white beard I used to like to stroke, and he called me 'Snickelfritz.'"

Scooter saw his chance to save his nickname from his mother's displeasure. "Scooter's not so bad compared to Snickersmits or whatever," he offered.

"No," she was still smiling as if she was remembering something nice. "I guess it's not as bad as if they called you Snickelfritz or, heaven forbid, T-Bone." At that they all had a good laugh in agreement.

"Well, speaking of T-bones, let's have a look-see at what I brought here," the grandfather said as he turned his attention to the boxes.

"Just a minute, Father Secory," Scooter's mother interrupted. "Gregory, you haven't had your breakfast. You sit down to some oatmeal that's made here.

Then you can go play or stick around, whatever you want to do, but you have to have your breakfast."

"Scooter, you're having oatmeal?" The old man began rummaging through his boxes. "You have oatmeal. . .I have. . .. Here they are. Raisins!" He broke open the package. "How about some raisins to spice up that oatmeal?"

"That'd be swell, Grampa. I'd like that!" Truth be told, Scooter was sick of oatmeal. Before his father lost his job, there would be eggs and bacon for breakfast several times a week, hot bacon grease to dip your bread in, and sometimes grapefruit to break up the monotony of oatmeal, Malt O' Meal, and corn flakes. But since his father lost his job, it had been oatmeal and nothing but oatmeal. The raisins in the oatmeal tasted almost as good to Scooter as the peppermint had.

His grandfather turned back to the boxes. "Let's see what we can find in here. I stopped by Dornbos Fisheries on the way out of town. They had good luck this morning and caught a ton of whitefish. They were asking only five cents a pound. Look in here, Ruthie," he said as he handed his daughter-in-law something heavy wrapped in brown paper. "I think there may be enough for a really nice dinner tonight. And they had some really good-looking smoked chubs I thought would make a nice lunch," he said as he continued to plow about in the box. "And I know you like cheddar cheese. I got this at the farmer's market this morning for a dime. Look at this," he continued as he undid the lid on a round wooden box.

Well, there was more food smells in that kitchen in a few moments than there had been in weeks. Scooter finished his oatmeal and slid off his chair and came over to the boxes to get a better look. There was a huge loaf of bread, blueberry muffins, a big tin of saltine crackers, two different kinds of cookies, a Mason jar of pickles, a package of raw chicken wings, a small ham, some snow peas, a head of lettuce, a head of cabbage and an apple pie. Grandfather Secory said he paid an Amish lady a quarter for it, but would get a dime back if he returned the lady's pie plate next week.

* * * * * *

The other players were already shouting, "First-ups," as Scooter left the kitchen to cross Century Avenue with his bat. Back in the kitchen, the older Secorys sat around the porcelain kitchen table, each savoring a cup of coffee. The perishable foods had been put into the icebox and the rest in the sideboard. Some of the cookies sat on a plate in the middle of the table.

After the sips from the hot coffee slowed and they had each had a cookie—well, little Russell had finagled two cookies from his grandfather despite his mother's warnings about spoiling the child, Grandfather Secory cleared his throat. "I hope you don't mind my barging in on you like this, unexpected and all. I tried to call, but your phone's been disconnected."

Scooter's father shrugged without looking up from his coffee. "It was something we thought we could get by without. Me without a job and no prospects in sight, we have to cut corners every which way and that was an easy decision, 'specially since they cut off the service for us not paying the bill."

"I figured as much. Well, the real reason I came by is since your mother died I find I can't manage the big house by myself. So I either have to find someone to move in with me or sell the house.

"And frankly, a second marriage is out of the question. I wouldn't want to associate with any woman who would lower herself to put up with a cantankerous old fool like me. So that leaves selling the place. I don't need to check with a real estate agent to know how that would turn out. The bank has foreclosed on so many places that it seems like there are more houses for sale in Grand Harbor than not. Plenty of places are just setting empty. So selling the place is not a good idea right now.

"Then I got what I thought was a brilliant idea. Why not find a nice family to move in with me? The wife could keep the house and do the cooking. I've got three big bedrooms I'm not using, and I rattle around in the place like a pebble in a tobacco can. No one to talk to, no one to eat with. . .." the old man grew misty-eyed. "Oh Peter, how I miss your mother." He took another sip of the coffee and wiped his eyes with his napkin.

"And then there's the widow Bach. She didn't wait until the grass grew back on your mother's grave before she made her intentions known." The old man raised his voice to imitate the old woman. 'Yoo-hoo, Merrill, have you tried my brownies? Yoo-hoo, Merrill, do you need any bread? I've just baked and have an extry lowaf! Yoo-hoo, Merrill, I have some of my delicious chicken dumpling soup if you'd care for it. I made a double batch.' It's 'Yoo-hoo, Merrill this' and 'Yoo-hoo, Merrill that.' God save me from that woman's clutches and her awful chicken dumpling soup. I think that soup may be the key to her husband's early death and why she never remarried." He paused to take a sip of coffee and to help himself to another cookie.

"So, I'd like you two to seriously consider helping out a lonely old man by moving in with me. I would be so grateful. My railroad pension is more than adequate to pay what few bills I have and to put food on the table. And here's the clincher. I told you I stopped by Dornbos Fisheries this morning. Well, my friend Lawrence has had a stroke of bad luck. His mechanic has been diagnosed with TB and will have to go to the sanitarium for anywheres up to three years.

"Lawrence asked what you were doing these days. I don't know what he'd pay, but we wouldn't lack for smoked chubs! You know he has six of them fishing boats to keep in repair now, and at least one of them is up on the sticks all the time getting refurbished or repaired. Nobody knows the diesel engines in them boats better'n you. What do ya say? Will the two of you help me put some life back in the old house and give a lonely old man a reason to live again? And above all, save me from the widow Bach?"

Chapter 3

Grand Harbor

When Scooter heard his mother call him in for supper that evening, he had just fouled off two sweet pitches. There was an imaginary runner on third, and Charlie Vanden Berg was on second. He was just one run behind Butch Minnema for the Championship of the World Series, so his playmates expected Scooter to stall.

Instead, he took off running for home. He had been thinking all day about the good smells in the kitchen after his grandfather arrived that morning. Then there was the smoked chubs on white bread with real butter that had been there for lunch. But supper was the moment he had been waiting for, World Series Championship or not. He knew that tonight's meal would be worth the sacrifice of beating Butch Minnema. There would be other World Series Championships won on the lot on Century Avenue, but tonight his stomach told him to take his bat and dash for home. And in spite of the protest of the other players (all except Butch Minnema), that's exactly what he did.

The smells from the kitchen were so good as he came through the screen door that he almost forgot to close it properly. But he remembered to turn and catch it just before the slam that would have created trouble for him.

Everyone except his mother was already at the table. She was in the process of taking a plate of something from the stove to the table. It was as he suspected. She had rolled the whitefish in raw eggs and cracker crumbs and pan-fried it. There were potatoes fried with onions, a bowl of cabbage salad, and a plate of thick slices of white bread.

"Just in time, slugger," his mother said as she put the plate of whitefish in the center of the table.

"That's Scooter, Mom," he said.

"Of course, dear. How could I have forgotten? After twelve years of calling you Gregory, I may slip back into Gregory a time or two," his mom winked as she sat down to the table.

"Let's bow our heads," his father said. Then he prayed, "For the bounty spread before us we are thankful, Heavenly Father. Bless it to our bodies and our lives to Your service. Amen."

Scooter knew that the chorus of "amens" that followed his father's were truly heartfelt. The Peter Secory family hadn't seen fresh meat of any kind for many weeks, so this was a feast, or bounty as his father had prayed.

Plates were passed. It was a rule in the Secory household that no one began eating until everyone had been served. Tonight that was hard to do, but it was almost enough just to smell the food and see it on his plate. And it tasted as good as it smelled when Scooter finally dug in.

There were just the sounds of eating for awhile. Forks tinkling against plates, Russell chewing with his mouth open. There was the crunch of cabbage salad and the sound of iced tea poured over chunks of ice that had been chipped off the block in the icebox. They were the sounds of good eating. Scooter was sure it was the sound of heaven after the hell of baloney sandwiches on old bread.

It was Grandfather Secory who broke the happy silence. He looked at Russell, pointed at the food on his own plate and said, "This is good junk, Maynard."

Russell grinned and looked around the table. "I'n not Maynard, I'n Russell."

"Oh, yes. I forgot. You're Russell. Well, it's still good junk, Russell." Then the old gentleman turned to Scooter. "Your mother called you Slugger when you came in to dinner. That was my idea. I was watching you play across the way there and from what I saw, I'm not so sure you should have corrected her. I think 'Slugger' would be an appropriate nickname from what I saw.

"On the other hand," he continued after a swallow of iced tea, "maybe it's not the kid with the bat in his hands, maybe it's the bat in the kid's hands, mmh?"

"Gee, Grampa, if it were just the bat, even Jinks could hit with it. But he can't hit for nothin'."

"Who's Jinks?" Scooter's mother asked.

"Wallace Jenkins. He lives on Hogan, down the block. He's in my grade, but he can't play very well."

"I'm not entirely sure I'm in favor of these nicknames," said his mother. "I think it's degrading. Why don't you just call him Wallace and have him call you Gregory?"

"Would you want to be called Wallace if you could be a Jinks?"

"There you have it," the grandfather interjected. "Put that way, there's no more argument for me. Given the choice, I'd rather be a Jinks than a Wallace any day."

"Father Secory! You're impossible." Ruth Secory tried to sound as if she was scolding the old man, but everyone knew she wasn't serious.

"I'd rather be a Jinks than a Maynard," said little Russell, and they all laughed except Russell who was puzzled.

"I think it's nice that you let Wallace play with you even if he isn't that good," Scooter's mother said. She was pleased to see Scooter accepting someone of lesser ability as an equal.

"We have to let him play. It's his ball. Besides, we can get him out easy, so he winds up being all-time fielder most the time. Jinks is okay."

His mother just raised her eyebrows and sighed, and his grandfather chortled behind his hand and then pretended to clear his throat to cover up his amusement.

The family talked and laughed as they passed plates and refilled glasses. Scooter was finishing off his second piece of whitefish when his father pushed his empty plate away from him with his thumb and cleared his throat. That was a sign everyone had better listen to what he was going to say.

"We have a family matter to decide, and I think it's important that we all think about what I'm going to say." He stopped and didn't say anything for awhile. Scooter suddenly realized his father had a lump in his throat—just like he had when he told

Scooter that his mother, Grandmother Secory, had died.

After a moment, his father was able to continue, but his voice sounded funny, like his words were going through a strainer. "Grandfather Secory has asked us to help him out. Since Grandma Secory died, he has had trouble keeping the house up and fixing meals and such. . .." The lump was back in Scooter's father's throat. Scooter glanced at his mother and was surprised to see her brush a tear away with her apron.

"Well," Mr. Secory continued, "he's asked us if we would be willing to come to Grand Harbor to help him with the house and there's a job - a good job for me at the place I worked at outa high school."

It was little Russell who saw it before Scooter did. "You want us live with you, Grampa? All da time? In your house? Can we? Wow!"

'Wow!' wasn't the way it struck Scooter when he realized what his father was saying. What struck him was a drowning, sinking feeling. His world was going down somehow. His school, his friends, his playmates, his neighborhood. They were all some-how detaching themselves from him and going down and around, out of his reach, and he was go-ing with them. It was like the swirling eddy that was formed when you pulled the plug out of the bathtub full of water and everything he knew was being sucked into it.

"Scooter?" his father's word brought him back to the table and the rest of the breaded whitefish on his plate. He suddenly had no appetite.

"Huh?"

"I asked you how you felt about it. You're part of the family, too."

"It's okay, I guess." Scooter couldn't help but say it in a way that told everyone else at the table that it wasn't okay. It was far from okay. Just like drowning wasn't okay.

"Well, I have an idea," his grandfather interjected, "Ruthie, why don't you cut all us menfolk a piece of that Amish lady's apple pie. I for one suggest a slice off that wheel of cheddar cheese on the top for those who want it. Then I have another idea.

"I'd like to take you all to Grand Harbor tomorrow. You haven't been to the place in awhile. Maybe we could pack a picnic lunch and go to the beach and take a look around the town. You don't have to decide tonight.

"Besides," and he leaned over to look Scooter in the eye, "I don't think some of us should make a decision about moving until they scout out the kind of baseball's played in the town and whether or not Grand Harbor could use a good player, the likes of which I saw play across the street this afternoon. What d'ya say?"

* * * * * *

Sleep didn't come easy for Scooter that night. Usually he would lie down and start thinking about the day's baseball game and be asleep before he knew it. But that night he couldn't even think about baseball. The thoughts of moving to a new place, a new neighborhood, a new school, a new city swirled in his mind. He wasn't sure he could find his way to his Grandfather's from the school, from the beach. And where would he go to school, and would he make friends or would he get beat up the first day? This was the scariest thing in his whole life. His chest became tight. For the first time in a long time, he buried his face in his pillow and cried. Bogeymen under the bed were nothing compared to this.

It must have been Gregory Peter who cried, because a Scooter would never cry, couldn't cry. Eventually, the activity of the day and the huge meal took its toll and he finally slept. But even his sleep wasn't a happy sleep. He woke up several times, even though he didn't have to get up to use the bath-room. Each time, the thought of leaving everything that was familiar to him came back and brought the pressure in his chest. Each time it was a while before he fell back to sleep.

Gregory Peter wasn't the only male member of the Secory family to cry into his pillow that night. So did Gregory's father. A letter had come in the afternoon mail from the bank. It said that if no fur-ther payments were made on the mortgage on the house and the back payments that had been missed were not paid up immediately, the bank had to fore-close. That meant the bank would put the house up for sale to pay off the debt the Secorys owed on the house. He knew it meant they would soon lose their house, just like they had lost their car.

Mr. Secory also knew full well that his father's request for help was not a request for help at all. His father was a resourceful man and could live by himself quite well. This was his father's way of of-fering to help his son help his little family. And Peter knew that he also had no choice. He had to accept his father's offer of assistance and the job in Grand Harbor. There were no jobs to be had in Grand Rapids. He had pounded the pavement for weeks for nothing. He cursed his luck through very real tears. At the same time as he cursed his luck for losing his job, he blessed his father for helping. Grandfather Secory had pulled Peter's little family out of trouble just like he pulled peppermints out of the children's ears. He truly was a magician.

Peter Secory, like Scooter, didn't have a happy sleep either. Partly because he was counting the bills he couldn't pay and the payments he couldn't make as if they were sheep to be counted. Partly because he could hear Grandfather Secory who was sound asleep on the living room couch, snoring like a buzz saw.

Grandfather Secory was sleeping the deep sleep of folks who were happy.

* * * * * *

It was early on Sunday morning when the dark blue Packard sedan backed out of the Secory's driveway on the corner of Lynch Street and Century Avenue and headed toward Grand Harbor. The sandlot was still covered with dew and it would be a few hours before first-ups would be called, this time without Scooter and his bat. Grandfather Secory turned left onto Century. Century Avenue ran parallel to the railroad tracks for several miles toward the center of town before it ran into Lake

Michigan Drive, which in turn was the road to Grand Harbor.

The mood that morning had been festive for Grandfather Secory and little Russell. For them, the day in Grand Harbor was an adventure. The mood of Scooter and his mom and dad was more somber.

It was Russell who, riding in the front seat on his father's lap, saw it first. "Whazat, Papa?" he asked, pointing to a jumble of wooden boxes and crates and canvas that had been assembled between the street and the railroad tracks and extended for nearly a half block.

"It's a Hooverville," his father answered. At that, Scooter sat forward in the seat to see what a Hooverville was.

"What's a Hooverville and who are those people there?" Scooter could see smoke rising from campfires and people lounging about wooden structures seemingly thrown together in a hodgepodge.

"Hooverville is a name given to these camps of people who have lost their homes or have gotten kicked out of their apartments for not paying rent. They've no money to get another place to live, so they make shacks out of discarded wood and crates and tar paper and such."

"They live there? In those shacks?"

"Yes, I'm afraid that's the only place they have to go."

"Why do they call it a Hooverville?"

"Because many people think that the Depression was caused by the policies of the President before Roosevelt—Herbert Hoover. These places have been called Hooverville, sort of in his honor, and the name stuck."

"There are kids in there!"

"It isn't just drunken old bums who are out of work. I heard tell that one of the guys I used to work with at Royal lives in there somewhere with his family."

Suddenly the reality of his family's financial plight became crystal clear to Scooter. They had lost all their money when their bank closed. Then his father lost his job, and then they lost their car. How long would it be before they lost their house, too? he wondered. As scary as it was to move, living in a Hooverville was a lot scarier, Scooter decided. He closed his eyes and sank to the back of the seat so he couldn't see the kids staring out of the tarpapered shacks at the shiny blue Packard going by.

His mother must have sensed what Scooter was

thinking because she reached over to squeeze his leg and whispered, "It'll be okay, Sweetie. I promise."

His mother's assurance did very little to take away the feeling that Scooter was drowning. His chest was so tight it was hard to breathe, and he had to fight to hold back the tears that were clawing their way through eyes clenched shut.

The ride to Grand Harbor took about an hour and a half on a dusty two-lane road. They passed fields being tilled with large draft horses hitched to plows. "Lot of these farmers are back to using horses," Grandfather Secory remarked at one point. "Ain't got enough money for gas in their tractors, if they haven't lost their tractors. Problem is there aren't enough horses to go around, so some are lending them out to others. You got to wonder how long this Depression is going to last and what it will take to pull us out of it.

"Just the other day, ol' Lester Fite told me his aunt's farm—twenty acres with a house and barn and all the tools – went for $200 cash money. All's they could get for it and were happy to get that. It's a goldarn shame, that's what it is. A fella can't go to the barbershop these days without hearin' someone or other's tale of woe.

Grand Harbor

"Look there, Scooter, there's the lake."

At that point the road dead-ended and connected
to another that wound its way along the shore of
Lake Michigan. In front of the car lay the wide ex-
panse of the lake. Its deep blue-green waters spread
out as far as you could see before the sky fell into it
far in the distance.

On other trips the lake had been a welcome sight
to Scooter. It meant Grand Harbor was just up the
road, and soon they would be in Grandma Secory's
kitchen where the smell of freshly baked pie and
chocolate chip cookies would greet them. And there
would be an outing on the beach shortly after. This
time there was no Grandma Secory, no smells from
the kitchen, no beach outing. There was only the
drowning feeling in Scooter's chest. And resentment
at Russell who didn't seem to realize the gravity of
their situation.

"Can we go to 'da beach, Grampa? Can we, huh?
Can we?"

"This is not where we go to the beach, little man.
But maybe we can go to the beach later. We'll see
what we have time for, okay?" the old man said as
he swung the Packard to the north and shifted
through the gears. "But one thing's for sure, we're
almost there."

40

We're almost nowhere, Scooter thought and again he had to stop breathing and clench his eyes shut to stop the tears that were fighting to get out.

They passed through forests of towering white pines and huge beech trees whose spreading branches formed a canopy over the road. They wove around the very steep sand dunes that were typical of the eastern shores of Lake Michigan. As they got closer to town there were fields of strawberries, asparagus, and blueberry bushes. Then the houses got closer together and they were in town. They turned onto Main Street with its small shops. There was the City Hall with the fire barn next to it. Funny, Scooter thought, they don't have horse-drawn fire wagons anymore, but they still call it the fire 'barn.'

They passed the First Reformed Church whose doors were open and Scooter could see a service in progress. They passed the Peoples Bank, Boer's Furniture Store, Mulder's Drug Store, and other shops all the way to the river where there was a wharf and big steamers tied up along Harbor Avenue. Grampa pointed out this store or that or waved to someone he knew. This was not the quickest way to his house and Scooter wished he would just get there and get the tour over with.

Grand Harbor

The old man turned at Harbor Avenue and followed the river toward the lake. Then turned again on a street that was unfamiliar to Scooter. And as they turned, his Grandfather said, "And this is Mulligan's Hollow on the right." Grandfather Secory turned and looked at Scooter, "And it's only two short blocks from my house."

Something in the old man's voice made Scooter sit up to look. It was a large flat area surrounded on three sides by high sand dunes. It might make for great sledding in the winter, Scooter thought. At the far end of the flat area he noticed about twenty small buildings. It seemed to be some kind of camp with the smoke from cooking fires floating lazily skyward. Scooter almost sat back down when he noticed some kids about his age on a grassy area across from the buildings. They appeared to be playing a game. Scooter couldn't tell what at first, until one of the kids picked up a bat. They were playing baseball.

Chapter 4

Dutchie

"I don't have anything in the house to eat without creating a stir n' a fuss," Grandfather Secory as they returned to Main Street. "So how about I take you over to Wally's Dee-lite Diner for some lunch?"

It had been months since Scooter had been out to eat in a restaurant. He looked up at his mother expectantly. She was smiling and nodded her head at Scooter.

Wally's had a long counter where a number of customers were seated on stools. The other side had tables and chairs with wire backs. "Morning, Wally." Grandfather addressed a tall man with a bushy moustache behind the counter.

"Morning, Merrill. Looks like you got your family in tow. Nice to see you all." He came out from behind the counter, past a glass case filled with cigars. "Everything we serve for breakfast is on the menu board over the counter there," his hand swept up to point to the big board behind the counter, then to another board on the back wall. "Lunch is on the back wall. Take your time. Lois will be your waitress. Just give a shout when you've decided. I favor the summer sausage sandwich myself. Make our own right here on the premises."

"That's what I'm having and a large stein of beer to wash it down," Grandfather Secory announced.

"Not today, you won't. You haven't been here on Sundays for a while. No beer or wine on Sundays in this county. You gotta be righteous on Sundays here whether you want to or not."

Scooter scanned the board. He saw that the summer sausage sandwich was ten cents, so was a large stein of beer.

"What's a BLT, Ma," Scooter asked.

"It's a bacon, lettuce, and tomato sandwich, sweetie."

That sounded good, but Scooter saw it was twenty-five cents, the most expensive thing on the board. To order the most expense item sounded piggy to him, so he announced, "I'd like the hamburger." The hamburger was only ten cents.

"The hamburger?" his grandfather asked. "What's not to like about a BLT?"

Scooter shrugged his shoulders. "I don't know."

"Ever had a BLT?"

"No."

"Then I think you ought to get a BLT. Expand your horizons. Whatdaya say?"

Scooter looked his father, wondering if it was okay and got a nod. "Okay."

Scooter thought the BLT was about the best sandwich he had ever tasted.

* * * * * *

When they had all finished, the old man paid the bill by leaving $1.35 on the table–$1.15 to cover their meal and $.20 for a tip. Then they piled into the Packard for the short ride to the Secory homestead.

Grandfather Secory's home was a wonderful collection of rich smells. Even if you were blindfolded, you could pretty much guess which room in the house you were in by the velvety fragrances. The kitchen, even with Grandmother Secory gone, still carried smells of baking. The living room smelled of furniture polish, and the dining room added a hint of silverware polish. The side room or sitting room where his grandfather smoked smelled of tobacco and leather. The upstairs bedrooms smelled of lilac from the sachets Scooter's grandmother had always kept in the dresser drawers.

The rooms seemed larger than life with very high ceilings and three section windows that went almost from floor to ceiling. The top section of the windows were made of geometric shapes - glass squares and rectangles with bevelled, or slanted, edges which were separated by channels of lead. When he was a small boy, Scooter liked to try and catch the rainbows that the sunlight made as it poured through the bevelled glass. The rainbows were elusive,though. If he tried to close his hand, the rainbow would slip through his fingers and land on his closed fist, or so he thought. The rainbows were also stubborn. They insisted on staying right where you found them, or so he thought.

This Sunday afternoon Scooter didn't see any rainbows, even though the sun streamed through the bevelled glass. Wrapped in his personal cloud of despair, he saw only the shadows which the lead channels made on the furniture.

Scooter heard his grandfather's voice coming from the side room. Merrill Secory was on the telephone with his friend Lawrence Dornbos, the man who owned the fishing trawlers and needed a diesel engine mechanic. "Well, he's here at my place now and I thought if you had a moment, he could meet you down at the boat dock and talk about it." Grandfather Secory paused to listen. Scooter could hear a man's voice squawking through the receiver, but couldn't understand what he was saying. The family sat quietly, waiting and wondering.

"I think that will be just fine. I'll send him over in my car. Thank you, Larry. I appreciate it." Then there was a pause and goodbyes were said.

"He just got home from church and he'd like to see you over there in a few minutes. He said he has to check the cooler before noon anyway. You take the Packard and get on down there and see what you can settle on," the old man said as he rose from the desk in the corner where the telephone had a place of honor.

Grandfather Secory handed the keys to the Packard to Scooter's father and wished him luck. Then he turned to Scooter. "It's too nice a day to be sitting around the house. Besides, there's something I want to show you. And then there might be time to saddle up one of the stools over t' Mulder's and get a phosphate or something. Whatdaya say?"

As sad as Scooter was, he couldn't help but be buoyed up by his grandfather's energy. And the thought of a soda at Mulder's Drug Store after he had already been treated to a restaurant lunch seemed unreal. He never knew what his grandfather had up his sleeves, but it was never boring.

As they headed for the back door, Grandfather Secory stopped on the back porch and picked a basket off a shelf. "We need to feed the chickens and gather the eggs first. If we leave the eggs in the nest too long, the layers will start to think of eggs as their own and we can't let that happen, can we?" He chuckled as he held the door for Scooter.

Merrill Secory's chicken coop was like that found in many backyards. There were eight to ten laying hens cooped in a pen that was attached to a small shed with nesting boxes. His chickens were red – Rhode Island Reds were their actual name. Grandfather Secory called them "Roadies" and was proud of the large brown eggs they produced, often with double yolks. The hens usually each laid an egg a day. If one of them neglected her duty for any length of time, her mistake could prove to be fatal. Instead of her eggs providing for breakfast, her grease would grace Grandfather's Secory's chin for supper. (She might end up on the dinner table.)

Scooter's grandfather handed him the basket. "You see if these old biddies have earned their keep. I'll get them some feed and check their water."

The chickens attended to, Grandfather Secory led the way down the driveway to the sidewalk. They turned left on 4th Street and walked briskly to Howard. A few houses down Howard Street Scooter spotted a boy about his age whittling on a large stick.

"Good," Scooter's grandfather said to him as they approached the whittler. "The Nagtzaam boy is home. I'd like you to meet him. I think you two have a lot in common." He raised his voice and addressed the boy sitting on the steps of his front porch. "Donny, how are you this fine day?"

"Fine, Mr. Secory. And thanks for askin'," Donny said has he got up from his pile of shavings.

"Whatcha makin'?"

"Trying to make a bat. Doolie Higgins got mad 'cuz Chappy Berilla struck him out so he smacked Woody Nelson's bat on the fence post so's he cracked it. The Nelsons got no money to get a new one, so I'm hacking away at this oak branch to see if it will work."

"Well, judging by the size of the pile of shaving, you're well on your way. I'd like you to meet my grandson, Donny, this is Gregory."

"How'd ja do. Actually my friends call me Dutchie. That's 'cuz folks call my old man 'Dutch.' Dutchie's sorta like being called Dutch Junior."

"Mine call me Scooter."

"Well, glad ta meechya, Scooter. You play ball?"

"I've got my own bat, but I don't have a mitt."

"Me neither, but if'n I had my druthers, I'd

ruther have a bat or a ball. You got a bat or a ball, they gotta let you play, right?"

"Listen, Donny–er–ah–Dutchie, Scooter and I were going to hike down to Ferry Field to see what's going on. Then we're gonna see if ol' man Mulder's got anything good at that soda bar of his. Want to come along?"

"Gee, I'd like to Mr. Secory, but I gotta ask my ma first. Can you wait a minute?"

"Be quick." Dutchie folded his pocketknife and bolted through the screen door. "Ma, Ma! Can I go with Mr. Secory to Ferry Field? Can I?"

"BAM!" the screen door slammed shut behind the excited boy only to burst open again as he came racing back through it. "I can go but my ma said I can't ask for anything." His rushed announcement was punctuated by another slam of the screen door.

"But would you take a peppermint if it was offered to you?"

"Sure!"

"Let's see. . . .." The old gentleman began fumbling through his pockets. "I thought I put them in this pocket. . .. No, not there. . .."

Here we go again, Scooter thought as he tried to keep a straight face.

"I'm sure I put a peppermint or two in my pockets before I left the house this afternoon." The old man went through his fumbling act, familiar to Scooter, but baffling to Dutchie.

Finally, apparently stumped, Grandfather Secory began his mumbo jumbo and his exaggerated gestures. He held out an empty hand and pointed to it with his other hand. "No peppermint here," he said. Then he swept his open hand around to point to the other hand which was also empty. "No peppermint here either. Now where did the peppermint go?"

That was Scooter's cue, "I just don't knoooow."

Grandfather then put his hand under his chin with his forefinger pointing to his nose. "I wonder where. . .oh, oh! I think I see it!" He reached dramatically behind Dutchie's ear. "There it was all along. Donny! All the while you let me fumble through my pockets and you had peppermints all the time!" The old man then reached behind Dutchie's other ear and pulled out another peppermint, "And you had one to share. Shame on you, Donald, befuddling an old man like that."

Once again the old peppermint trick worked. This time Dutchie just stared at the old man in amazement. "How'd you do that?"

"How'd *I* do that? How'd *you* do that? How do

you hide such big peppermints in such little ears, I'd like to know. Do you want both of these peppermints or share with Scooter?"

"Share."

"Here you are, Donald, and one for you, Scooter. But be careful, there might be ear boogers on 'em."

Dutchie was dumbfounded and looked the peppermint over carefully before popping it into his mouth.

The walk to Ferry Field took them down tree-lined streets where Grandfather Secory pointed out where the foreman of the tannery lived, where DeBoer the dentist lived, and where old man Robbins lived. At other houses, Dutchie pointed out yards where he and his friends snitched grapes or apples every fall. Scooter noticed that a number of houses had vegetables growing in their front yards instead of grass.

"This here's where Doolie Higgins lives. He's the biggest bully on the south side, but he can play ball real good, ya gotta give him that," Dutchie said pointing to a large red brick house.

"Is Doolie his real name?" Scooter asked.

"Naw, Doolie comes from his middle name which is Doolittle."

"So he must be the son of Doc Higgins, then?"

Grandfather Secory asked. "And his mother was Clara Doolittle who passed away some years ago?"

"Yep, Ma says Doolie's mean 'cause he lost his ma to TB when he was little. All's I know is if'n you call him Lester, you better be ready for to get a whuppin' laid on you. He don't like anyone callin' him that."

"Is Lester his real name?" Scooter asked.

"Yep, and he's real twitchy about hearing it. I seen him take off across the playground at Central School when he heard a kid calling him Lester. Lucky for the kid he was a good runner. But I heard that Doolie knew the kid and caught up to him later and laid a whuppin' on him 'til he cried."

Just as Dutchie ended his tale about Doolie Higgins, Scooter heard a crowd cheer somewhere up ahead and noticed there were a lot of cars parked along the street.

"What's that cheering, Gramps?" Scooter asked.

"That's probably coming from Ferry Field. It's something about Grand Harbor I wanted to show you. It's a real baseball park, and local factories have teams that play here on the weekends. It's called Independent Ball. I think this afternoon the Story and Clark Stringers are playing Keller Tool." The old man was interrupted by another chorus of shouts and cheers.

Dutchie broke into a run. "C'mon, Scooter, let's see what's going on," he shouted over his shoulder.

Scooter looked up at his Grandfather.

"Go ahead with Dutchie. I'll catch up and find you."

Chapter 5

Ferry Field

Ferry Field was exactly like a field out of Scooter's dreams. He had seen pictures of the Major League baseball parks like Briggs Stadium in Detroit where his beloved Tigers played. There were newsreels in the movie theaters that showed Babe Ruth hitting home runs in Yankee Stadium. But this wasn't a photo or a darkened theater. This was bright sunlight, and the players weren't moving about herky-jerky like in the movies. This was real.

There was a very high fence for a backstop to corral foul balls and foul poles rising above outfield fences. There were dugouts where the players sat in front of bleachers down sidelines full of people. The grass in the outfield was perfectly flat and ended abruptly on the perfectly flat sandy infield with real base sacks. Players in uniforms were just coming off the field toward one dugout, and players from the other team were coming out of their dugout to take positions in the field. From the scoreboard Scooter could tell that Story & Clark was leading Keller Tool by 3 -1 after three innings.

"C'mon, there's no one sitting on the sand box!" Dutchie said as he led Scooter to a large wooden box with a metal cover that sat just off the field past third base. "C'mon, climb up. This box is where they keep the extry sand for the infield. It's a great place to sit to see the game, and we can fetch foul balls," he said.

"Do you get to keep the foul balls?" Scooter asked as he climbed atop the box.

"Naw, but it's fun to shag 'em down and throw 'em back to the field. They're real baseballs, ya' know, just like in the Major Leagues—all nice an' white and they got a sweet feel to them. It's great just to hold one. Ever see a real professional ball?"

"No. Mostly we play with an old taped-up ball. Kid in our neighborhood had it. He wasn't any good, but we let him play 'cuz he had the ball."

"Well, here sometimes we're lucky and a ball goes into the bushes in ol' lady Wampole's yard back there," Dutchie said pointing to a fenced yard well down the foul line. "She's a mean old crab and won't let kids in her yard to fetch 'em. Claims we step on her tomato plants or whatever. So if one goes in there and she doesn't see it, we can wait until dark and sneak in and get it. Sometimes if a ball gets scuffed too bad, they'll take it out of the game and give it to the Boy Scouts for our games. Then if one gets too bad for the games, Mr. Farley will give it to us to play with at school or at the Hollow."

"Are you a Boy Scout?"

"Sure, aren't you?"

"No."

"We play our games against other troops. Mr. Farley is our assistant scoutmaster and our coach. He plays here for Miller's Dairy."

"Does your mother let you go out after dark–to get balls from the backyard over there, I mean?"

"Naw. She'd never let me do that. WAY TO GO SMOKIN' JOE!!!" Dutchie screamed so suddenly and so loudly it startled Scooter. A batter had just struck out swinging, and there were similar shouts from the crowd.

"Do you know that pitcher?" Scooter asked in amazement.

"Course. That's Joe Durkins. He lives just down the street from me. He works at the piano factory. They gave him a job and moved him here from Chicago just because he's a great pitcher. Good hitter, too. I bet he could play for the Detroit Tigers if'n he had the chance."

"The piano factory?"

"You know, Story and Clark. They make pianos."

"Oh."

The next batter swung at the first pitch and hit a high foul ball that the catcher caught. Two out.

"If your ma doesn't let you out after dark, how do you get the baseballs from the yard over there."

Dutchie didn't answer for a moment. He fiddled with his shoelaces and tied his shoe in silence. Then he turned to Scooter. "If'n I tell you, do you promise not to tell anyone?"

"Promise."

"Cross your heart and hope to die?"

"Promise. Besides, who could I tell? I don't know anyone here."

"Your parents, dummy. No one can know this or we'll never get any more balls."

"I promise."

Dutchie lowered his voice. "See that house with the red shutters across the street behind the other dugout?" he whispered.

"Yeah." Scooter found himself whispering back even though "yeah" was no secret.

"That's where Beans Mulder lives. He plays on my Scout team. The window on the side of the house is his bedroom. He sneaks out at night after he's supposed to be in bed and gets the balls."

"You play with a kid named Beans?

"His real name is Harley. You don't gotta wonder why we call him Beans."

Scooter thought for a moment and did wonder. "Why?"

"Would you like to go around bein' called Harley?"

"No, I guess I'd rather be called Be. . .."

"LOOK OUT!" Dutchie interrupted. "Here comes a foul ball!" He clamored off the box and raced to retrieve a line drive foul that had whizzed over their heads and landed in some tall grass outside the ballpark fence. Scooter was not far behind, and they both were well ahead of several boys who came out of the bleachers to pursue the foul ball.

Dutchie had gotten a line on the ball when it bounced into the tall grass and he pounced on it almost immediately. "Got it," he said triumphantly, holding the ball over his head.

"Good job," Scooter said and turned to go back their box seat.

"Great seat, ain't it? Wanna hold the ball?"

"Gee willikers, can I? Don't you have to throw it back?"

"Not until the end of the inning. They have other balls. Here. Take a look, but I get to throw it back. I found it."

Ferry Field

Scooter had never held a new ball in his hands before. In fact, he had never seen a new, white baseball before. He was surprised how light it was and how smooth the seams were. "Wow," he whispered under his breath. "You could throw a ball like this a mile and hit it even farther." All the balls he had played with were either dirty brown or wrapped up with black tape with strings showing through the cracks in the tape.

* * * * * *

Although Keller had tied the game in the sixth, the Story & Clark Stringers won 5-3 on the strength of Lefty Schmitter's two-run home run in the seventh inning. The foul ball score was three for Dutchie and one for Scooter. The highlight of the game for Scooter was throwing the foul ball he found in to the third baseman, because the game was out of baseballs. He almost felt like a player. "Nice throw, kid," the third baseman had said.

As they walked away from Ferry Field Scooter reminded his grandfather of his promise to make a trip to Mulder's Drug Store.

"Sorry, Mr. Secory. I can't go with you. Ma says we don't trade on Sundays."

"Well, Donny," the old man answered. "I'm sorry

you can't go along, but I respect your parents for
that. Perhaps we can do it another time?"

"I'd like that. Well, I'll just run along home. It's
almost time I got to bed anyway. See ya later,
Scooter. Nice to be shagging fouls with you." At that
he broke into a run for home.

"What did he mean he doesn't trade on Sundays
and why is it nearly his bed time?" Scooter was
puzzled.

"His family takes a dim view of stores being open
and buying things on Sunday. Sunday is for church
and family times, not for commercial purposes. So
there aren't many stores open hereabouts on Sunday. There are a lot of Dutch folks in Grand Harbor, and they're good people. They work hard and
take care of their property. Generally, they don't go
to movie or dances, but they go to church twice,
sometimes three times on Sunday. And they don't
like other folks drinking beer on Sunday either.

"And the reason Donny needs to get to bed early
is because he has to be to his uncle's house at two
in the morning. He works on a fishing boat."

"He works for money?"

"Actually, I don't think he gets paid very much,
maybe nothing. But he gets a big breakfast every
morning and he gets to keep some of the fish that

can't be sold. That puts food on the table. His dad
got hurt and can't do much physical labor and had
to take a job as a flagman on a WPA project. He
only makes $10 or $12 a week. So Donny does what
he can to help out. Lot of families like that."

The walk to the drugstore took them to Main
Street and past one darkened store after another
until they got to the corner of Third and Main where
the drugstore stood like an oasis in a wasteland.
Scooter went for some empty stools at the counter,
but his grandfather talked him into sitting at one
of the few tables for two.

"What'll it be, Mr. Secory?" a skinny kid with a
Coca-Cola hat asked from behind the bar.

"I'll have one of your famous chocolate malteds
with chocolate ice cream, and my young friend here
will have. . . ?"

"I've only had an ice cream cone here before.
What else do they have?"

"Anything you ever heard of or can think of, kid,"
the skinny kid answered. "But I'd recommend a lime
phosphate. Best in town, guaranteed."

Scooter looked at his grandfather as if to say,
"What's a lime phosphate?" The old man nodded
his head and winked knowingly. "Lime phosphates
were your grandmother's favorite. I think you'll like

it."

"Okay, I'll have one of those lime. . .thingies."

"One chocolate malted with chocolate ice cream and a lime thingy, coming right up."

Upon hearing "lime thingie," a girl at the counter sputtered and sprayed a mouthful of ice cream over the counter before she could get her napkin up to cover her mouth. At that, they all had a good giggle.

After the treats came and Scooter had a chance to taste his lime thingy and declared it "gee-willikers-good," his grandfather looked at him with studied eyes.

"Scooter, I think I know how much you don't like the idea of moving away from your school, your neighborhood, and your friends. When I was a boy about your age, I had to leave Germany with my parents and brother and move to Chicago. We had to move for pretty much the same reason as your pa and ma have to move. There was no work in Germany and we were down to eating rotting potatoes out of garbage dumps. My father had a promise of a job in the slaughter houses in Chicago just like your pa has the promise of a job here." He took a long suck on his straw, swallowed and then said, "Ahh" appreciatively.

"Seems to me, you can look at this in two ways.

One is that it's a terrible thing to have to move here, and it's going to be nothing but miserable for you. Or you can look at this as an opportunity for you. It is a tremendous opportunity for your pa and ma to get back on their feet financially. It's an opportunity for your family to help me out in my old age with your grandma gone, and it's an opportunity for you to meet new friends and have new experiences.

"I've found in my life that outcomes have more to do with attitude than with circumstances. To put that another way, it's not the hand that's dealt you, it's how you play the cards that determines whether you win or lose."

"What kind of new experiences?" Scooter asked cautiously.

"Well, for one thing, I know that the Boy Scout troop down at church could use a good hitter on their baseball team. They have a lot of games left this summer. You could play in real games as well as play a lot of work-up at Mulligan's Hollow. There's a lot of great kids in our neighborhood, kids like Donny Nagtzaam. I'd like you to give it a real try. I just know you'll like it here a whole lot," the old gentleman took another tug at his straw.

"Just like I know this chocolate malted beats

rotten potatoes in Germany or anywhere else," he said with a twinkle in his eye. "Whatdaya say? Keep an old man company. I promise to come to all your baseball games."

With that the old gentleman took a coin purse from his pocket and counted out twenty cents for the drinks and a nickel for a tip. "I see you have a little bit to go on your lime thingy. Sit here and finish up while I go to the back counter for some cigarettes. I'll be right back, and then we should skedaddle for home."

Chapter 6

The New Neighborhood

When Scooter and his grandfather got to back to the Secory homestead, there wasn't much doubt about whether they would move. It was just a matter of when. Peter Secory had accepted the job at Dornbos Fisheries as a mechanic repairing boat engines.

"How's the money?" Grandfather Secory asked as the family sat down to enjoy a piece of warm-out-of-the-oven apple pie made by Scooter's mother in hopes there would be something to celebrate.

"Forty-six cents an hour for forty-eight hours. Nine-hour days plus three hours on Saturdays. It's a higher rate than I made at Royal Machine, but the hours are less.

"So it's about the same paycheck for less hours. I'll have to be on call during off hours. A fisherman can't afford to have his boat tied up for too long.

"For all the places I've been to looking for work over the past months, actually begging for a job, any job, to walk into Dornbos' and get a job just like that. . ... I'm afraid I'm going to wake up and find out this is a dream." Peter Secory grinned, and suddenly Scooter realized he had not seen his father smile for weeks.

Merrill Secory knew it wasn't a dream. He and Dornbos were old friends, and Merrill had lent the fisherman money to buy his latest boat. What Peter Secory didn't know and would never find out was that there were several qualified candidates for the mechanic job at the fishery. Peter had moved to the head of the line because of his father's business relationship with Lawrence Dornbos.

"Well, that's great news," Grandfather Secory said as he squished down on the last crumbs of his pie to force them into the tines of his fork. "Scooter and I had a great afternoon as well. Saw a ball game down to Ferry Field, then whet our whistle at Mulder's. All in all, I think Scooter might be ready to sign on with the church's Boy Scout baseball team as a shortstop. So it 'peers to me the only thing left is to get you moved in and make this old house come alive again."

* * * * * *

The move had taken a full two days. They could only find a small trailer to borrow, so it took four trips. With each trip the Packard and the trailer were loaded to the maximum, and on the last trip they even had boxes tied to the running boards.

It was Wednesday morning during a breakfast of bacon and the Roadies' double yolkers that Dutchie showed up on the back porch. He was with another kid about the same age, but smaller.

"Donny! Come on in. Who's your friend? Looks to me like it could be the Nelson boy. Is that right?"

The Nelson boy nodded.

"And your name would be Woodrow. Is that right? If you're not a spittin' image of your pa, I don't know who or what is. Do your friends call you Woodrow?"

"Woody."

"Well, Woody, meet my favorite grandson named Scooter. Gregory is his nickname. His real name is Scooter. For the life of me I can't figure out why anyone would want to be called Gregory if they could be called Scooter. I think Scooter is a fine name, don't you?"

Both Donny and Woodrow smiled at the old man's prattle. But he continued. "How comes you aren't out with your Uncle Brum this morning, Donny?"

"We're back in early. A strong northwester came up sudden like, and we had to get off the lake real quick. Only got about a third of our nets up and almost didn't make it back to the pier heads in time. We came to see if Scooter wanted to play ball down ta the Hollow."

"I'm finished, Gramps. Can I be excused?"

"You go, slugger. Show these boys what a Secory's make of, okay? And I wanna hear all about it when you're back for lunch. Every pitch, ya hear?" He had to shout the last words to Scooter's vanishing backside.

"Zat yours?" Woody wanted to know, looking at Scooter's bat as they made their way to the Hollow.

"My pa made it for me."

They walked for a bit in silence.

"Can I try it?"

"Sure." Scooter handed the bat to Woody.

Woody gripped it and waggled it back and forth. "It's a little bit too heavy for me. I'll be having to choke up on 'er. But it's a sweet bat with your name and all on it."

"Thanks."

"Wonder who will be there this morning?" It was Dutchie wondering.

"How many do you usually have," Scooter wanted to know.

"Anywheres from eight to fifteen or so. If we

have fourteen, we choose up sides and play teams. Listen," Dutchie said, directing their attention to some shouts coming from the Hollow . "There's kids there already. Let's go." He broke into a run for the half a block to Mulligan's Hollow, with Scooter and Woody on his heels.

When they got to the field, there were only six other kids there. Dutchie introduced Scooter to all of them. "That's Casey, this's Red, Slats, Stoney, Packy, and Chappy. This here's Scooter." There were nods around.

"Not enough for teams," Chappy ventured.

There was an awkward silence for a few moments, which Scooter broke. "Do you do first-ups or Ibbidy Bibbidy?"

They all looked at Scooter as if he were an alien from another planet. "We do first-ups and we were waiting for someone to call it so we could get dibs. But what the heck is Ibbidy Bibbidy?" Dutchie asked.

"It's a way to do first-ups without the shouting and screaming," Scooter replied. "I'll show you if you want."

"First-ups isn't so bad if'n Doolie's not here, but show us the ibbidy bibbidy thing."

"You all stand in a circle around me and hold

out your fists, sorta like you were holding candles."
They all did as Scooter said. "If one of your fists
gets the k'nahbull, put that fist behind your back.
First guy with two k'nahbulls is first up. Ready?"

"Wait a minute. What's a k'nahbull?" Casey
wanted to know.

"You'll see." Scooter started with Dutchie and
gently slapped his fist and then each fist in order
as he intoned the words, "Ibbidy, bibbidy, sibidy,
sab; ibbidy, bibbidy, k'nahbull." The word k'nahbull
came on Stony's fists and Scooter directed him to
put it behind his back, leaving him with only one
fist in the circle. Then Scooter continued around
the circle, "Ibbidy, bibbidy, sibidy, sab; ibbidy,
bibbidy, k'nahbull," and another fist disappeared.

Stoney was the first one with two fists behind
his back, so he was first to bat. Casey was second.
Slats was the pitcher. Scooter, as the k'nahbull
caller, was automatically the first baseman, Woody
shortstop, Packy the left fielder, etc.

"Hey, that's neat," Dutch said admiring. "Never
heard of that before, but it beats having to outshout
Doolie."

"Do you play pitcher's hands?" Scooter asked.

"Yep, pitcher's hands. . .."

"And automatic second. . .."

"And force at the plate." Nearly everyone chimed in. Scooter nodded that he knew the rules. First, a batter was out if the pitcher got the ball in his hands before the batter reached first. Second, if a batter reached first safely, he was automatically awarded second base safely. Then, a runner on base had to reach home plate before a fielder in possession of the ball could touch the plate.

"I call hitters-getters," Woody said, which meant a hitter was responsible for retrieving any foul ball he hit way out of the field. Everyone nodded assent.

"And I call dibs on bats and mitts," Casey called and everyone looked at Scooter.

"Dibs on bats and mitts" was a new one to Scooter, so he just shook his head and shrugged his shoulders at the same time.

Slats sensed Scooters confusion. "It means that if you didn't bring a bat or mitt, you can use another guy's if'n he's not using it. You got the only bat, but no mitt. I have a mitt, but no bat. You get dibs on my mitt when I'm batting, and I get dibs on your bat when you're not batting."

So that's the way it works, thought Scooter. If you have the only bat, you have the power. You can trade the power for another kid's mitt if he's batting. "'S'okay with me," Scooter declared.

With rules understood and agreed to, the game began with Stony at bat and Slats pitching.

Stony got a single and automatic second. Casey tripled Stony home. Stony flyed out to Red, so he went into the outfield and Slats went up to bat and Scooter became the pitcher.

Slats left his mitt on the mound for Scooter to use. It was a beauty—a Lou Gehrig pro model. Scooter took a moment to savor the feel of the soft leather and the smell of the linseed oil that had been applied to keep it soft. A kid could catch almost anything with a mitt like this, thought Scooter. A kid wouldn't mind being all-time fielder if he had a mitt like this.

Slats hit Scooter's first pitch—a little squibbler that Scooter was able to pounce on before Slats got to first. That meant Scooter was batter and had to leave the precious mitt.

For some time Casey, who had yet to be put out, and Scooter were the batters. Scooter sensed it was important to make a good impression on his new friends, so he waited for good pitches. When he hit the ball, he ran like the wind. Finally he was forced out at the plate when Casey hit a ground ball to Slats at shortstop who fielded the grounder cleanly and beat Scooter to the plate.

Just then a large boy came down from the street with two other boys in tow. From the way he walked and the way the other two boys treated him, Scooter could tell he was somebody used to getting his way.

"There's enough for teams now," the big kid said as they approached the field.

"We're playing work-up, Doolie," Slats said. "Eleven ain't enough for teams," Slats continued, "You want to play, you go to the outfield like everbody else. You're behind Scooter."

This must be Doolie Higgins, Scooter thought, and instinctively picked up his precious bat to protect it. He noticed one of the new boys was barefoot.

"What if I don't want to?" Doolie snarled.

"Less'n you got your own bat and ball, I guess you won't be playing," Slats replied, although not forcefully.

There was a moment of awkward silence as Doolie looked around as if to size up his odds. Then he spotted Scooter and his bat. "Who's this kid and whose bat?"

"This is Scooter and it's his bat. Just moved from Grand Rapids," Dutchie said.

"Well, ain't that just peachy. We got a new kid

and he's got a bat. L'see the bat, kid—Scooter or whatever they call you," and he reached for the bat.

Scooter held it out to him.

Doolie took the bat and took a practice swing with it. "It's okay, I guess."

Dutchie took a few steps toward Doolie. "Mind you, don't break it over the fence post like you did Woody's. If'n wasn't for Scooter's bat, we'd be hitting with sticks."

Wow, thought Scooter. Dutchie, you're brave.

"And what if I do, Dutchie? Whatcha gonna do about it, huh, Fish Breath?"

"What part of the Boy Scout Law do you get, Doolie? Or is that just when you put on the uniform?" Scooter could see Dutchie's remark stung.

"Woody's bat was gonna break anytime anyway. All's I did was tap that fence post. Besides, it was too small anyway," he replied weakly as if he didn't believe his own excuse.

"Yeah, well, it wasn't too small for Woody. You should learn to treat other people's property with respect, that's all's I'm saying. Now you can go to the outfield and play or go home. We don't got enough for teams."

"I say we got enough for teams!" Doolie was adamant. It appeared Doolie had no intention of going in the field and working his way up to bat.

The situation was saved as three more kids came down from the street. "Now we got fourteen. That's enough for teams. First choice!" Doolie cried out, triumphantly.

The work-up game was over and the players began choosing sides. Doolie and Dutchie chose for the teams. Doolie chose the barefoot kid first, a boy he called Red. Dutchie chose Slats. Doolie chose Bub, the other kid that had come to the field with him, and Dutchie chose Scooter. Doolie chose Casey, and they continued to alternate choices until all the kids were chosen except Woody.

"Ha, ha," Doolie snickered and then said in a mocking voice, "You have to take Woodrow."

"You got first choice, so we get first-ups," Dutchie said.

"First choice is first-ups," Doolie countered and moved toward the plate as if to lead his team to bat.

"Is that the way you do it in your Boy Scout troop? Is there a merit badge for being able to get your way by being the biggest, Doolie? What does that badge look like, huh? Is it a picture of a big fist smashing a little kid? Do they call it the Bully Badge?"

There was a tense silence as they all waited to see whether Doolie would kill Dutchie or just hurt him real bad.

But Doolie tossed the bat down and started to take the field. "No need to get your knickers in a knot about it, Fish Breath. C'mon guys, let's kick the crap out of these whiny little wimps."

Scooter heaved a sigh of relief as the game began. There was such admiration for Dutchie from this teammates for standing up to Doolie that he got to bat first and be the pitcher without any challenges.

Things went smoothly for quite a while. All the outs were clear. There were no close plays. The smoothly part stopped after several innings, however, when Doolie came to bat. He hit a long foul ball to right field that went far enough to go over a small depression and roll some distance towards the barracks used for CCC workers.

Hitters-getters had been called so Woody, who was playing in right field, didn't move to get the ball. Another tense silence descended on the field. Doolie stood at the plate leaning on Scooter's bat.

"Woodrow," Doolie finally said in a mocking tone. "Aren't you going to fetch the ball? We ain't got another that I can see."

"Hitters-getters," Woody said in a shaky voice.

"Nobody called hitters-getters. You're in the field, get the damn ball, you little wimp."

"Your troop give badges for cussin', too, Doolie?" Dutchie asked. "Must be you don't wear any of these badges of yours 'cuz I ain't seen many badges a' tall on your sash at the last Jamboree."

"Shut your face about the Scout crap or I'll shut it for ya, Fish Breath," Doolie snarled.

"You ain't smart enough to know when to shut your own mouth, Doolie. I can't think you know how to shut someone else's. We called hitters-getters before you got here. So you get on your horse and get the ball, so's we can finish whuppin' on your sorry team. Or are you scared I'm gonna strike you out?"

"You couldn't strike a match, Fish Breath," Doolie sneered. "Now tell your wimpy friend to get on his horse and get the ball or I'll pound pebbles up his pants."

"You get the ball, Doolie. It's hitters-getters and you know it. There hasn't been a time you've played here that it wasn't hitters-getters. We'll wait."

All Scooter could think about was the story of Doolie breaking Woody's bat over the fence post for striking out. Striking out was nothing compared to this, and his precious bat was resting in Doolie's hands.

Doolie shifted the bat, waggled it with both hands, and looked defiantly at his opponents. The fence post that had proved fatal to Woody's bat was about fifteen steps behind Doolie. Scooter was about twenty-five steps from Doolie.

"I'll get the ball," Scooter said quickly and turned to race after it.

"Smart kid," Scooter heard Doolie say.

The game broke up at the sound of the noon whistle atop the Story & Clark factory building and the topic of conversation on the walk home was Doolie Higgins.

* * * * * *

Lunch was liverwurst sandwiches with white cheese and mustard and cold white milk. And however liverwurst sandwiches might have sounded to someone else, it didn't sound like oatmeal to Scooter or to little Russell either. As Grandfather Secory said, "It's good junk, Maynard."

"So tell me, how'd the baseball go?" Grandfather Secory asked. "Remember, I want to hear all the details. Did you get any hits?"

"Yep, in fact they never got me out and I never had to use automatic second. We had mostly littler kids, but some of them were really good. Casey, Dutchie, Slats–they're all real good players."

"Couldn't we please refer to these boys by their given names? I'm not at all in favor of these nicknames as I think I've said a time or two before." Scooter's mother was exasperated .

"But Ma, I don't know their real names and everyone else calls them by their nicknames. I'd be the only one except'n Doolie. He calls kids by their first names to mock them. That's what kid's 'ud think I was doin'–mocking 'em."

"Well. . .," Mrs. Secory wasn't entirely convinced.

"So you had a good time?" asked Grandfather Secory to change the subject back to baseball.

"Mostly we had fun."

"Mostly? What about the not-so-mostly part?"

"Doolie Higgins showed up and caused some trouble. But Dutchie stood up to him. The game almost ended when he wouldn't do hitters-getters."

"What in the world is hitters-getters?" Scooter's mother wanted to know.

"The kids that hits it, gets it, like foul balls that get hit way off in the boondocks. Doolie hit a foul ball that went almost all the way to those buildings in the Hollow. . .."

"The CCC barracks. The young men living there

are earning money for their families by planting trees south of town."

"Yeah, the barracks," Scooter continued. "We had called hitters-getters and he wouldn't get it. I was afraid he'd get mad and break my bat like he broke Woody's, so I went and got the foul ball."

"Sounds to me like young Higgins is not a very nice boy."

"He's not, Ma. He called Dutchie 'Fish Breath' and cussed and everything."

"Well! That settles that. You're not to play with him. I won't have you hanging around riff-raff that breaks other people's things and calls them names and swears. We don't need to be associating with him and his kind."

"Hurrumph. . .hack." Grandfather Secory cleared his throat, warning his daughter-in-law not to carry this too far. "I'm not sure we should make a blanket statement about his kind. I b'lieve this young man's father is Dr. Higgins. In fact, he's the doctor who treated Grandma. He's a fine doctor and a real gentleman. Hear tell, the boy is out of sorts from losing his own mother at an early age. But I support your mother, Scooter. I found it's best not to associate with bullies and idiots. First they drag you down to their level, and then they beat you with experience."

"But Dutchie really put him in his place. Really he did. When Doolie swore, Dutchie asked him if his scout troop gave badges for swearing and Doolie didn't swear again."

"So young Mr. Nagtzaam put him in his place, did he? Apparently he's one that's not afraid of the Higgins boy," said Scooter's mother.

"Oh, he was scared, all right. We were all scared. But Dutchie's father told him that bullies are often escared themselves and if you stand up to them, they'll turn tail and run." Scooter paused to take a drink of milk. "What's a badge, Grampa? And what's a sash?"

"I believe you mean merit badges? Mmm. I'd be happy to tell you what I know. But why do you ask about merit badges? What does that have to do with Donny and the Higgins boy?"

"That's how he stood up to Doolie. Asked him if his troop gave merit badges for being a bully and for swearing."

"I see. And that put young Mister Higgins in his place did it? Well, good for Donny. Who'd a thunk it? I suspect that as with most bullies, if you look way down deep, Doolie's bluster is really shallow." The old man looked at Scooter to see if he got the play on words, but Scooter's expression didn't change. Then he continued, "Well, Scooter, merit badges are awarded by the Boy Scouts after a scout completes study or an activity in an area of interest. I'm not aware of all the badges, but I know, for example, a fella can get a badge in canoeing, in swimming, in life saving, tying knots. . .all kinds of things. And a sash is like a big ribbon you wear that holds all your merit badges.

"But why am I trying to explain this? I know a fella who knows all about scouting, and especially their baseball program. I think we should go meet him after lunch. We can take the Packard 'cuz he lives across town near the tannery. And I hear tell he could use a good hitter on his Scout troop's ball team. Whatdaya say?"

Chapter 7

The Boy Scout Troop

Scooter was bringing his lunch dishes to the sink when he thought he heard someone singing. The voice was coming from the street. It was a man's rich baritone and he was singing . . .no. . .calling or chanting at the top of his lungs. Scooter turned to look at his Grandfather to see if he heard it, too, and the old man's eyes were smiling.

"That's the huckster," the old man said, anticipating Scooter's question.

"What'th a huckthter?" little Russell wanted to know. So did Scooter.

"It's a man with a truck that sells fruits and vegetables up and down the streets. He bellers out like that to let the housewives know he's in the neighborhood so they can come out and look over his wares. He'll beller again in a few minutes. See if you can understand what he's saying."

Before long the singsong cantor of the peddler started again, this time right in front of the house:

ToeMAYtoes and poTAYtoes,

Come SEE here VHAT vee GOT.

Vee SELL dem BY da PENny,
SELL 'em BY the LOT!
All are FRESH, none are OLD,
YOU can Trade in penNIES,
but they're VURTH their
VEIGHT in GOLD, yah!

"It's old man Burgess. Ruthie, come on, let's see what he's got on his truck today. Scooter, watch he keeps his thumb off the scale." With that, they all scampered for the door.

It was a horse-drawn wagon fitted with a rack that had shelves sloping away from the center and others which hung out over the wagon's sides and back. Hanging from one of the shelves was a large scale used to weigh purchases. The shelves were mounded with vegetables and the floor of the wagon was covered with potatoes and turnips. All along the street women came out from their houses wearing housedresses and aprons and carrying their change purses. Scooter's mother bought some green beans and a head of cabbage, spending ten cents for the lot.

"What did you mean, 'watch he keeps his thumb off the scale', Gramps?" Scooter asked as they headed back toward the house.

"Mr. Burgess has a heavy thumb, and sometimes

when you buy things by the pound, you pay for his thumb as well."

"He thells you hith thumb?" little Russell asked incredulously.

"No, he applies a little pressure to the scale with his thumb as he weighs your vegetables. So if the scale reads two pounds, you aren't getting two pounds of beans, you're getting one and a half pounds of beans and a half pound of thumb."

"Oh, I get it. In other words, he cheats," Scooter said matter of factly.

"Only if you catch him.Once the widow Bach nailed him dead to rights by re-weighing five pounds of potatoes when another customer distracted him. The five pounds she had purchased had mysteriously shrunk to four and a half pounds when his thumb wasn't on the scale. Only the offer of a free melon saved her from calling the cops.

"C'mon. Get in the Packard. Let's go see the Scoutmaster."

* * * * * *

George Ryan McHenry was the paymaster at the tannery, and because he had to work Saturdays to pass out pay envelopes, he had Wednesdays off. They found him trimming the hedge in front of his neat bungalow. He had close-cropped gray hair and a pencil-thin moustache that matched. His features were sharp and everything about him was in perfect place. His shoes shined so that you could see your face in them.

McHenry straightened up from his clipping when the Packard pulled up, and he approached the car when he recognized Merrill Secory as the driver. He held himself ramrod straight, but Scooter noticed that he walked with a limp; one knee didn't seem to want to bend.

"Good day to you, Merrill. How is retirement treating you?"

"Beats riding the rails, George. And how are you?"

"I feel a change in the weather coming in the old knee, but other than that—can't complain. Who do we have here?" he asked, addressing Scooter.

"I'd like you to meet Gregory Secory, who goes by the name of Scooter. Scooter, this is Mr. McHenry." Scooter reached out to shake Mr. McHenry's extended hand.

"From all the great things your grandfather's been saying about you, I expected someone much bigger." Mr. McHenry said it so seriously that Scooter couldn't tell if he was serious or kidding.

"Sorry, sir. This is as big as I can make me for right now."

"Well, from what your grandfather says, it'll likely be enough. So you like to play baseball, do you?"

"Yes, sir."

"Are you a Boy Scout?"

"No, sir. We didn't have Scouts around my place in Grand Rapids."

"How old are you, son?"

"Twelve."

"Would you like to be a Scout?"

Actually, Scooter knew he would do anything to play real baseball with teams and umpires, being a Boy Scout was an added bonus. "Yes, sir!" he replied.

"Very well, Gregory. You have your grandfather take you to the church basement and see a Mrs. Overbeek. She'll see you get a Boy Scout Handbook. It will tell you what you need to know and do to become a Scout. Now let's see, I think the Troop has a baseball practice tomorrow at the field on Seventh Street at 6:30. Do you think you can be there?"

Scooter looked at his grandfather who nodded his permission. "Yes, sir!"

The Boy Scout Troop

* * * * * *

The basement of St. John's Episcopal Church was a busy place. There was a large room that had racks of clothes of all sizes and kinds where people seemed to be shopping. Mothers were holding things up to children for size. One rack of children's clothes had a sign that said "Central," another rack said "Ferry," and still another had "Spring Lake" scrawled on it. There was a shelf with a few used shoes.

There was another room that had cans and boxes of food, soup, and other things. A lady with a list was putting items into a sack. This was the lady that Scooter's grandfather was looking for. "Mrs. Overbeek? George McHenry directed me to see you about getting my grandson here a Boy Scout manual."

"I think we can arrange for that," she said to Mr. Secory. Then she turned to Scooter. "Have you done your good deed for the day?"

Scooter didn't exactly know what that meant, but he knew he hadn't done anything special for anyone yet that day. "No, ma'am."

"Well then, you can begin your Scouting career by carrying this sack of canned goods to the other room for me. Then if you gentlemen will follow me please, we'll see about that Scout manual." She led the way to yet another room that had a rack of green uniforms and other Boy Scout paraphernalia. A sign on the door read "B.S.A. Troop 23. Grand Harbor, Michigan."

"Do we fit him up with a uniform as well?" Grandfather Secory asked.

"We can get him a uniform, but he's not to wear it until he is a Tenderfoot," the lady answered as she handed Scooter a small blue book with a picture of a Boy Scout on the cover. "Technically, a boy is not a Scout until he passes the requirements to become a Tenderfoot. Learn the motto, know the flag, and learn to tie a few knots. All you need to know is right there in the handbook. Mr. McHenry's good about helping you. Then, when you pass the requirements and become a Tenderfoot, you get to wear your uniform and badge."

* * * * * *

"How come's they had all those clothes and food in the church basement, Gramps?" Scooter asked when they were back in the Packard heading home.

"That's all food and used clothes that people donate to the church. Folks who's on hard times can come and get what they need for their families."

"What did the signs mean?"

"What signs?"

"One rack of kids' stuff said 'Central,' and I ferget what the other ones said."

"Oh, those signs. They tell what school the kids went to that wore those clothes. So if your child goes to Central School, you might pick things from another rack so when she goes to school she won't sit next to the kid who wore the same clothes last month."

"There were a lot of people getting clothes."

"These are tough times. Read in the paper just the other day that one out of every four families have lost their jobs. Your papa was lucky his job lasted as long as it did, and now he's got another one. I know some men who have been out of work for two years.

"Just last week I drove down the alley behind Wally's Dee-lite Diner over on Main Street and saw the Presler kids eating out of the garbage barrels. In fact, I know Wally takes special care of the leftovers folks leave on the table and puts them out for the Preslers and others that come by and pick them over. Some folks say they're looking for scraps

for their dog. I 'spect their kids see the scraps before the dog gets a sniff of them, and that's all he
gets - a sniff.

"Here we are," he said as he turned into his
driveway. "Let's get inside and see if your ma ap-
proves of the fit of your new uniform."

Scooter wondered how close he had come to eating out of garbage barrels and his chest got all tight.
But he didn't cry. This time the tightness didn't
come from being scared. It came from being grateful to this wonderful man who was setting the park-
ing brake on the 1936 Packard.

* * * * * *

In his excitement to play real baseball, Scooter
had overlooked a problem. He didn't have a mitt.
Surely the team needed a bat and he had the best
bat he'd ever hit with, but what if he needed a mitt
to play? The question bothered him to the moment
he showed up at the Seventh Street field.

There he found Scoutmaster McHenry with a
clipboard and a list of some kind. Standing with
him was a younger man. There was another
younger man sitting on the grassy rise nearby.
Scooter thought he looked familiar.

When Mr. McHenry saw Scooter he waved him

over. "Here's young Secory now," he said to the younger man. "Gregory, this is Mr. Farley, our Assistant Scoutmaster and baseball coach. Farley, this is Gregory Secory, Merrill's grandson recently relocated from Grand Rapids. His grandfather tells me he's played a bit of ball so let's see where we can use him."

"Yes, sir. How do you do, Gregory, is it?"

"My friends call me Scooter."

"Then Scooter it is. I like the sound of that name. You get it or earn it?"

"Got it mostly, but it stuck." Scooter was finding this man easy to talk to.

"What kind of ball did you play in Grand Rapids."

"Just work-up."

Roger Farley frowned as he looked at the kid in front of him who had no mitt, was a bit small for his age, and had no real baseball experience. "Scooter, huh." He seemed to reassure himself that someone with the nickname of Scooter should be a good player.

Scooter sensed the coach's doubt. "We didn't have Boy Scout baseball where I lived. All's we had was work-up, but I've played for three years now."

"That's great, kid. We'll work you in

somewheres." Scooter could see the doubt lingered and decided this wasn't the time to tell the coach he didn't have a mitt.

Scooter looked around. He spotted Slats, as well as Stony who was throwing to Chappy. The red haired kid who had played on Doolie's team and had no shoes was there. He was still without shoes and was playing catch with his bare hands. As Scooter looked over the kids, Woody rode up on an old bicycle.

"Scooter, you gonna' play for us? Are ya?"

Scooter nodded.

"That's swell. He's good, Mr. Farley, real good. And can I use your bat? He's got a really great bat, Mr. Farley. Too big for me, but better'n the ones we got." Woody's pleasure at seeing Scooter seemed to put words in his mouth.

"That's great, Woodrow," Mr. McHenry said. "Now just you stick close by here," and Mr. McHenry raised his voice, "I have some announcements, boys. Please gather round and be at attention." He paused as the team gathered around him.

"First off, I'd like to introduce you to Gregory Secory who will be joining our troop playing for our team. I expect you to introduce yourselves to him and make him feel welcome.

"Better call him Scooter or he won't know yer talking to him," Slats interjected.

"Thank you for that observation, Mr. Slatski. Now I have the floor, if you please." He paused to let his authority sink in, then continued, "or even if you're not pleased. Now then, if I'm allowed to continue—as you may know, the July Fourth holiday falls on a Saturday this year. In fact, it's the Saturday following this coming Saturday. The Scoutmasters have agreed to have a baseball tournament in the morning here at Seventh Street Field. The teams that will be participating are First Reformed, First Methodist, St. Pat's, the Lutherans, Troop 24, and ourselves. Miller's Dairy is treating with lemonade and ice cream after the games, and members of the winning team will be awarded a ribbon. Any questions?"

Woody's hand shot up.

"Yes, Woodrow?"

"Are we still going to march in the parade?"

"Yes, Woodrow. This doesn't relieve us of our obligation, our privilege, actually, of marching in the parade. Nothing further, then?" There were no more questions.

"They're all yours, Mr. Farley."

"Thank you, Mr. McHenry. Okay, boys. Our

record so far isn't anything to brag about. One win and three losses. I don't think we're hitting as well as we could or should. So I've invited Smokin' Joe Durkin who plays Independent Ball for Story & Clark to help us with our hitting. So here's what were gonna do tonight. I want you all to take the positions you had at the last game, and we'll get you up here one by one to take a few licks. Smokin' Joe will see if he can't make big leaguers out of the lot of you. So off you go then."

Most of the players trotted off to take up positions in the field and the young man who had been lounging on the grassy knoll got up and came over to Mr. McHenry and Mr. Farley. So! The young man Scooter thought he recognized was Smokin' Joe Durkin. Scooter didn't have a position to go to, so he stayed put.

"Who's my first victim, Roger?" Smokin' Joe asked.

Mr. Farley saw that Scooter was the only one still standing nearby. "You, kid, Gregory. You swing first."

Scooter looked at Smokin' Joe. "What do you want me to do?"

"Just get up to the plate and swing at the pitches like you usually do."

As he walked to the batter's box, Scooter looked to see who was pitching. Slats. Good. Scooter had batted against him in a work-up game that morning. Slats could throw strikes, but Scooter had hit well against him.

Slats' first pitch was high and Scooter let it go by. The second pitch was right down the middle, and Scooter hit a hard grounder that got between the third baseman and Red, the kid with no shoes, who was playing shortstop. Scooter looked up at Smokin' Joe.

"Hit a few more, kid."

Scooter got back into the batter's box and Slats threw him another strike. This time Scooter smacked a line drive right over Slat's head. When the ball had been thrown back to Slats, Scooter dug in again. This pitch was wide of the plate and Scooter let it go by. The next pitch was a bit high, but Scooter managed to get good wood on it and sent a high fly ball to left, which the left fielder caught.

"Not bad, kid," Smokin' Joe said as he approached the plate. "I bet you get a lot of hits, but not many homers, am I right?"

"Wow! I wonder how he knew that?" Scooter thought.

"Am I right?" Smokin' Joe repeated himself.

Scooter nodded his head. That was right all right.

"That's because you're using your arms for power, not your legs, and you're hitting with your weight behind you. You are able to hit well because you have great hand-eye coordination. But you could be a lot better.

"Here's what I want you to do. Instead of standing with both feet together, leave your back foot where it is but move your front foot about twelve inches to your left. Have your feet about as far apart as your shoulders. Then take a big step toward the pitcher as you swing. That way you will be forced to step into the pitch more, and you will be getting more power from your legs. Try it."

Slats next pitch was right down the middle again, and Scooter swung and missed. The new position didn't feel right, and he looked up at Smokin' Joe. "It feels funny."

"I shouldn't wonder. But doin' it wrong just because it feels better than doin' it right is no excuse. Take a couple'a practice swings first to get the hang of it and then try it again."

Scooter did and with each practice swing, it did feel more comfortable. He stepped back into the batter's box. Slats gave him another pitch right down the middle. Scooter swung and connected, this time, as Smokin' Joe predicted, with much more power and the left fielder watched it sail over his head.

"See what I mean, kid. You keep working on that and I think you'll have a lot more power."

Scooter snuck a look at Mr. Farley and was pleased to see a big smile had replaced the look of doubt.

Scooter's smile was bigger.

Chapter 8

The Perfect Mitt

It was almost dark before Scooter got home the night of that first practice. He, Slats, Stony, and another kid everybody called Hammy had stayed at the field after the practice ended and kept on working on the things Smokin' Joe Durkin had told them. Scooter's mom was sitting in the living room knitting and listening to Major Bowles Original Amateur Hour on the radio while his father and Grandfather Secory were in the side room. Scooter could hear them talking about the new job at the fishery as he poured himself a glass of water.

"So, how'd it go, Slugger?" Grandfather called when he heard the faucet running. "Wow, Gramps. They had Smokin' Joe Durkin there and he watched me hit. He told me to adjust my feet, and now I can knock the cover off'n the ball. It really helped me. He helped ever' body. He showed Slats how to rock off'n his back leg and throw the ball a lot harder. He showed Hammy how to take a bigger step toward the plate when he pitched and he can throw strikes a lot better now. I can't wait 'till a real game."

Scooter's father looked up from the cigar box he was rummaging through. "Who's Smokin Joe Durkin?"

"I understand he's actually a Chicago boy," Grandfather Secory said. "Story & Clark brought him up here and gave him a job if he would play on their ball team. I hear tell he's a pretty good pitcher. We saw him beat Keller Tool just the other day, didn't we Scooter?" The old man paused to light a cigarette.

"Scooter, look what I've got here," Scooter's father said with wonder in his voice. Scooter could see the cigar box he held was full of cardboard cards with pictures on them.

"What are they?" Scooter was about to ask and then he understood. "Baseball cards! Wow!" There were dozens and dozens of them. Right on the top was Walter Johnson and Ty Cobb and a Cy Young and there was a Christy Matthewson. "Geeeee willikers! Where'd you get these, Pa?"

"They're your grandfather's."

"Actually I've been smoking Piedmonts for twenty-five years and these cards starting appearing in the packs. I kind of liked them, so I just started tossing them in a cigar box. Some of the others came in Cracker Jack boxes, some in caramel candy packages. There must be two, three hundred of 'em. That's only one box. There are two more boxes of them in the attic."

"Do you got a Babe Ruth?" Scooter wanted to know.

"You know, I don't think I ever got a Ruth Card. But these days, cards only come in bubble gum packages and my store-boughts don't cotton to bubble gum."

"Store-boughts? What are store-boughts?"

"He means his false teeth," Peter's father replied.

Scooter was enthralled with the cards. Kids at his school in Grand Rapids had cards, but he didn't know anyone with this many. There was a Rogers Hornsby, a Shoeless Joe Jackson, another Ty Cobb. Tris Speaker, Pie Traynor, Johnny Evers– Scooter recognized most of the names. "Whatcha gonna do with these cards, Gramps?"

"Well, there was a time when another young feller about your age would play with them by the hour. He'd line them all up according to teams." Scooter looked up at his father who was smiling.

"Great way to play baseball on a rainy day," his father said. "But there was only one box of them back then. There's a whole lot more of 'em now."

"So now whatcha gonna do with 'em, Grampa?"

"Well, I was waiting for just the right fella to come along who I knew would take real good care of them. Someone who liked baseball so's I could find 'em a good home. For right now, why don't you play with them if you like—'til we find the right fella, that is." Scooter could tell by tone of the old man's voice the right fella had just been found.

There was a momentary pause as Scooter fingered through the cards. Then Grandfather Secory spoke.

"Scooter, your father and I were wondering what you are doing for a mitt?"

"I borrow from other kids. They use my bat, I get dibs on their mitts."

"Do you have any idea how much a mitt costs?"

"No. I hear tell most kid's parents can't afford them, so I suppose they cost quite a bit."

"Well, listen. You go in the living room and in the magazine rack, you'll find your Grandma's Sears and Roebuck Catalog. Get it and let's see just what it really would cost."

Scooter just sat still looking at his grandfather. Could it be he could pull mitts out of a kid's ear like peppermints?

"Well, aren't you going to get the catalog?" his father nudged him with a stocking foot. Scooter set his glass on the coffee table and went into the living room toward the magazine rack. As he reached for the catalog, his hands trembled.

The baseball gear was on page 687 and there were several mitts, including the Lou Gehrig Professional baseman's model that Slats had. It was $4.69, a lot of money. It was $4.69 more than Scooter had. He had no idea gloves cost this much. Scooter was focused on the impossibility of ever owning a glove when he heard his grandfather talking to him.

". . .happened to hear that Mr. Cashmere at the grocery story down on Main and Seventh needs a reliable delivery boy from three to six in the afternoons on weekdays. Pay's twenty cents a day plus what a kid might pick up in tips. But the boy has to be twelve. Too bad you're only eleven."

Eleven? He was twelve. Or was he still eleven? No, he was twelve. "But I am twelve. . ." and then he saw the smile start to crinkle the lines around the old man's eyes. "Gramps! You know I'm twelve."

"You're twelve? I thought you were only eleven. Well, then, maybe you could qualify to be this delivery boy. How long would you have to work there to be able to send for a mitt?"

A job? A mitt? How long? Scooter's head was so muddled, he couldn't give an exact answer. "More than four weeks, that's for sure."

"By that time baseball will be over for the season," his father said.

"But I could use it in work-up for the rest of the summer and then I'd have it for next year's games."

"Well, we were thinking that no self-respecting Secory ought to be playing baseball bare-handed. So we thought that if you were willing to go get the delivery job, maybe we could loan you the money for a mitt. Then you could repay us with your delivery money. Which mitt do you fancy?"

Scooter didn't plan on playing first base, so the Lou Gehrig baseman's mitt was not really what he needed. The Mel Ott Professional fielders glove was a lot cheaper at $3.29 and could be used anywhere on the field. It would be perfect.

* * * * * *

Scooter couldn't get right to sleep that night. The highlights of the day were replayed on the screens of his closed eyelids. A real practice, the ball sailing over the left fielder's head, the image of Smokin' Joe Durkin, the smile on Coach Farley's face, the Sears Catalog, the baseball cards which

had a new home under his bed, a Mel Ott Professional model mitt. The more he thought about that
mitt, the mitt that would soon be his, the tighter
his chest got. This time he let the tears come out.
They were tears of joy, and he wasn't the least bit
ashamed of them. He wasn't even bothered by the
wet spots they were making on his pillow.

Scooter snuffed his nose. He turned his thoughts
to the work-up game that he would certainly be part
of at the Hollow tomorrow morning. But he was
asleep before Ibbidy, Bibbidy had selected the first
batter.

* * * * * *

Scooter could hear a parrot shrieking. It seemed
to have invaded his dreams. No, it wasn't in his
dreams, it was real, and it was coming from downstairs. Someone was in the kitchen with his mother.
By the light coming through the shades, Scooter
decided it was time to get up anyway.

When Scooter entered the kitchen, an old lady
was having coffee with his mother and grandfather.
"Ah, good morning, Scooter. This is Mrs. Bach, our
neighbor. She brought us a batch of her delicious
sugar cookies. Wasn't that nice of her?" his mother
said.

"Scooter? Did you say his name was Scooter?" the old woman cackled. "That's not his real name, I hope. It's as bad as the Stinson boy. They named him Sylvester. Never liked the name Sylvester. The kid turned out as bad as his name, if you ask me. He's the one they caught stealing cigars from Sporty's Bar, ya know. Red-handed, mind you, in broad daylight. Hear tell he just helped himself. And him only fifteen. His father's as bad. Never did a lick' a honest work in his life, to my way of thinking. How he has the money to have whiskey on his breath all the time is beyond me. You know," she said lowering her voice, "they're the ones who ate their dog a while back. I know times is tough, but to eat your own dog. . ."

"Scooter," Mr. Secory interrupted the widow's chatter. "You need to get going. You haven't had your breakfast yet, and I think we're out of eggs. Let's you and me gather the eggs so's your mother can fix breakfast." Scooter's grandfather got up from the table and headed for the back door. "Don't let me stop you two ladies from catchin' up on the news. C'mon Scooter, we got chores to do." Grandfather Secory was out the back door with Scooter only too happy to follow.

What an annoying voice, Scooter thought as

they approached the chicken coop. It was shrill and harsh and came from the back of her throat.

"That woman grates on my nerves like a cat sharpening her claws on a screen door. Her mouth goes like a whippoorwill's. . .ah, tail. And it's sharp enough to cut through fog. Every time she says, 'if you ask me,' I'd like to chime in and tell her I didn't ask and I'm not going to ask, so don't tell me."

"Did those people really eat their dog, Gramps?"

His grandfather stopped and turned to him. "That's what people say, and the dog hasn't been seen since the gossip started. But if they did, they did it to stay alive and it isn't any of anyone else's business but theirs. Furthermore, I'm suspicious of how the good widow Bach gets close enough to Judd Stinson to know he's got whiskey on his breath. Maybe we should ask her that, heh?"

He returned to his job of getting the chicken feed. "I've half a mind to go down to Wally's for breakfast, but I feel bad leaving your ma alone with that old crone. Ah, quiet. Don't look up and act busy," the old man had lowered his voice. "She's leaving now and with any luck, she'll. . .drat it all! She's comin' for us. Is there no escape from this woman?"

"How many layers you got now, Merrill? I know

you're partial to Rhode Island Reds, but I favor the Brown Leghorns myself. They're not as fleshy, but I think they're better layers and I have them for the eggs, of course. Much easier to feed. Sometimes I think they'd get by on grass and sand if ya didn't feed them. 'Course the Reds have brown eggs to the Leghorn's white. Some say the brown eggs are better for you, but I don't find that, do you? An egg's an egg, I always say. I see the Freemans got rid of their layers. I don't think they ever had good luck with them, did you? Do you know what breed they were? Looked like a sad mix of goodness knows what to me. And that rooster they had! Sorriest excuse for a rooster I ever saw. Couldn't even crow proper, if you ask me. . ."

No, Scooter agreed, there was no escape except perhaps the path her first husband chose. Eat her chicken dumpling soup and die.

* * * * * *

"I don't mind her," Ruth Secory said when they finally sat down to their breakfast. "She does talk a lot. She fancies your electric refrigerator. She still has an icebox. I think I can tell you all about it if you care to hear. Couldn't stop talking about how lucky Mother Secory was to have a refrigerator over her icebox. She's a lonely old woman. It's the least we can do to be kind to her."

"I find I can be kinder to her from a distance and the farther, the kinder," was all Grandfather would say. Then he changed the subject to Scooter's job interview at Cashmere's grocery store.

"If Mr. Cashmere gives you the job, you have three choices. You can do the job poorly and you won't last a week. Drop the lady's eggs or crush her bread or steal so much as a cookie crumb, and she'll ring up Cashmere before you're out of her driveway and all her neighbors next. You can do a passable job and you'll keep it 'til some kid hungrier than you proves to Mr. Cashmere he can do it better. Do a bang up job and someday you'll own the store. Every housewife you deliver to will form an impression not only about you, but also about Mr. Cashmere and about your family.

"Having said all that, I wouldn't have recommended you for the job if I didn't think you'd be a credit to yourself and Mr. Cashmere. So good luck and off you go."

"Wait a minute," his mother stopped him before he got to the door. "Let me look at you." She straightened his shirt, fussed with his hair, and re-snapped a suspender that had come crooked. "I can't let you go for your first job looking like I don't take proper care of you. There, that's better," she said as she spun him around for his grandfather to approve.

"Go get'em, Slugger," his grandfather said. "And remember, don't drop any bread or squeeze any eggs."

* * * * * *

"So, you're Peter Secory's boy." Mr. Cashmere was a heavy man with mutton chops, or bushy sideburns that came well below his ears. He draped his rotund body with a soiled butcher's apron. He wore a straw boater that had a red, white, and blue stripped band. He looked down at Scooter over a bulbous nose. "You're kind of small. Are you fast?"

"My friends call me Scooter."

"Okay Scooter. Here's the deal. Lot of housewives call late in the afternoon for things they need for supper. That's why I need someone just from three to six, ya' unnerstand? They call for a loaf of bread, some sugar, or some pork chops, mebbe. And they think they need it yesterday. So we got to get it to them Johnny-on-the spot, know whadda mean? Ideally, they'd like it delivered over to them before they hang up the phone. Do you think you could do that?"

"I'll try."

"You'll try. Ho, ho. That's a good one. I think we'll get along just fine, Scooter. He'll try. I'll have to remember that one. Dollar a week is all I can pay, and I pay on Monday for the week before. Do you have any questions?"

"Do I collect money from the people I deliver to?"

"Oh my, no. Most of my customers have accounts with me. They trade here and I keep accounts and they pay me on payday, some ub'em end of the month, so you don't have to worry about collecting. 'Course I got some accounts that ain't paid in awhile. I'd like you to collect those for me. Do you think you could do that?"

"I'll try."

"You'll try. There you go again. That's great, Scooter. You come back at three, and we'll send you scootin' all over town. We'll give you a try for a week, then we'll talk again next Friday and see how you're doin', and if you like it enough to give up your afternoons to be a working man."

At that the jolly man turned and picked an apple out of a bin and polished it to a waxy shine with his dirty apron. "Here. It's on me. If I hear a customer say you got her order to her before she hung up the phone, you get another one." And with that he waddled back toward the meat counter chuckling to himself "I'll try, he sez," and Scooter had his first job. He was so proud, he thought his chest would burst. A job, an apple, and soon, a Mel Ott Professional Model mitt.

As Scooter went out the door, the word BASE-BALL on a handbill on a telephone pole caught his eye. He went over to read it:

BASEBALL

THE GRAND HARBOR
INDEPENDENT ALL-STARS
VS.
THE PITTSBURGH CRAWFORDS
Champions of the Negro
National League
featuring Satchel Paige, Josh
Gibson, and "Cool Papa" Bell

7:00 P.M. FRIDAY EVENING JULY 3
AT **FERRY FIELD.**
Admission $.50. Children
accompanied by an adult are free.

Scooter walked briskly toward the Hollow hoping he might get in on the tail end of work-up before the noon whistle. As he walked he thought about the handbill. The game was next week Friday. If he could only talk his father and grandfather into going to see the All-Stars play the Pittsburgh Crawfords. What a game that would be!

Crunching on his juicy, crisp apple as he walked along, Scooter spotted Red—the kid who never seemed to wear shoes.

"Red! Red! Wait up!" called Scooter as he broke into a run. When he caught up to him, he asked, "On the way to the Hollow?"

"Yeah. Nothing else to do."

"Me, too." Scooter took another bite out his apple.

"I'm glad you're gonna join our troop and play for us."

"Ain't never played real baseball before, with real balls and teams and umpires and stuff."

"I like it. 'Ceptin we haven't won much. Doolie's team mercied us last Sattaday," Red acknowledged.

"Mercied? What's mercied?" Scooter took another bite of his apple.

"If one team's ahead by more than ten runs after five innings, they call the game over 'cuz of the ten run rule."

"But why to they call it mercied?" Scooter noticed Red looking at his apple, which had only a few more bites to the core.

"Because to end the game, the umpire mercifully puts the losers out of their misery." Then Red paused. "Whatcha gonna' do with your core?"

The question puzzled Scooter. He was about to say, "Throw it away, of course," when he realized why the boy was asking. "Actually, I'm full. The rest is yours if'n you want it."

"Sure," was the quick reply. The shoeless boy took what was left of the apple, twisted out the stem, and as they walked he ate the whole thing—core, seeds, and all.

Chapter Nine

Play Ball!

Scooter was able to get only a few chances to bat before the noon whistle ended the game. Actually, his heart was not in the game. All he could think about was Red eating the apple core. Scooter recalled that it wasn't so long ago that he didn't know if he could face another meal of oatmeal. But now he was living in the lap of luxury with meat at every meal, while his new friend was one of the many victims of the Depression.

Scooter had just taken an automatic second when an idea struck him. Maybe there was a way to help Red. At the sound of the noon whistle, it was time to put the plan into action. Red did not hurry off the field as the others had, and Scooter hung back himself.

"Do you have any baseball cards?" Scooter asked him.

Red looked up with interest. "Yeh, some. My aunt gets 'em in candy packages or gum or something. She saves them and gives them to me. She just has little kids."

"Got any Babe Ruths?"

"One. Mebbe two. I'm not sure."

"Wanna trade him?" Scooter asked.

"I dunno. What'd ya got?"

"My grandfather gave me a bunch. Why don't you come over and see? Maybe we got something you don't. We could do it right now."

"I don't know. It's dinnertime. Don't you have to get ta eating?" Red asked.

"Maybe you could eat at my house, and we could look at the cards after."

From the look in the shoeless boy's eyes, Scooter knew it all. The question was would hunger overcome pride? He wondered if anyone had ever seen that same look in his eyes.

"Okay, if'n your ma won't mind."

"Naw, she won't mind. C'mon. I'll race you to the street."

When they got to street they had to stop to avoid running into the iceman's wagon. "Let's go beg chips!" Red said. Mr. Kelly, the iceman was just unloading a 25-pound block of ice with his tongs as they approached.

"Got any chips, Mr. Kelly?" Red asked.

"You two are sweating up a storm. Whatcha been doing? Playing baseball at the Hollow?"

"That's jest what we're coming from now and we're awful hot," Red said in an exaggerated pleading voice.

"Well, I can't let you wilt down to nothing right here on the street. Would a sliver tide you over 'til you can make it home for a cold drink? Let's see." He reached into the back under the tarp covering the wagon and came out with two shards of cold clear ice. "This do?"

"Thanks a lot, Mr. Kelly."

"You're welcome, boys."

* * * * * *

"Gramps, Ma, this here is Red. He's come to see our baseball cards. He's got a Babe Ruth. Maybe he'll trade."

"Well, well, look's to me like it's the Van Dorn boy." Scooter's grandfather seemed to know everyone. "Seems like I see you in the fourth row of church most every Sunday."

"Yes, sir."

"Well, young Master Van Dorn," Scooter's mother interjected. "What's your name? I don't abide these awful nicknames. I bet you have a perfectly good first name."

The red-haired boy hesitated. "Ever' body calls

me Red, Ma'am. Even my ma."

"That's all well and good, but around here we try to call people by their given names. Not by Doolie or Slats or whatever. So what's yours, sweetie."

"Percival." There was an awkward silence. That was even worse than Harley. "It was my grandfather's name. They call him Percy and they call me Red 'cause of my hair. If'n it's all the same to you, Ma'am, I'd druther be called Red.

"Well, all right then. Red it is," she conceded, remembering something she heard not long ago: *Would you want to be called Wallace if you could be a Jinks?*

"Well, Scooter, tell me. How did you and Mr. Cashmere get along?" his grandfather asked.

"I'm on trial for a week. I'm to start today at three o'clock."

"That's great," and with that his grandfather turned the conversation to their guest. "Well, Red, how's your pa? Is he still laid up from the car accident? Terrible thing. Ruthie, I think we're going to have a guest for lunch. We're having some fresh smoked chubs. You like smoked fish, Red?"

"Yes, sir. But if you don't mind, I have to ring Mrs. Denton to tell my ma I won't be home. Else she'll be worrying, and I'll catch heck when I do get home."

"You just set here at the table and dig into those chubs and white bread. I'll ring up Mrs. Denton for you," the old man got up from his seat and went into the dining room to make the call.

"Who's Mrs. Denton?" Scooter wanted to know after the food had been passed.

"They live next door," Red said between chews. "We ain't got a phone no more. Denton's got a kid our age. Bub plays for the Troop 24, with Doolie."

"Was that the kid that came to the Hollow with you and Doolie the other day?"

"Yeh, that was Bub," Red replied after a long drink of his milk.

"Scooter, Dutchie, Beans, Red, Doolie, and now Bub. Will we ever get to the point of calling our young men by their proper names?" Scooter's mother said with a note of exasperation in her voice.

"What would you say if people named their children Scooter and Dutchie and then called them Gregory and Donald? Would you insist on Scooter and Dutchie then?" Grandfather Secory said as he came back from the dining room. "Mrs. Denton said she's sending. . ." The old man paused so as not to offend Scooter's mother. "What's the Denton boy's real name–Percival?" he said as he sat down at the table.

Red thought for a moment as he chewed, "I don't rightly know. He goes to Catholic School. I go to public. Less'n you go to school with someone and the teacher says it, you never know their rightful name. All's I ever know'd was Bub. That's what his ma and pa call him, too."

"Well, whatever his name, you're covered with your ma," the old man said. He reached for the plate of smoked chubs. "Had your fill of these smoked fish yet, or will you try another?"

"I'll have another, if'n you've plenty." There was plenty. And the boy with no shoes had another and another.

* * * * * *

When the meal was finished, Scooter asked if they could be excused to look over the baseball cards.

"Yes, you can. But before you go to Cashmere's this afternoon, I have a small chore for you to do," Grandfather Secory instructed. "There's a bunch of old newspapers in the corner of the garage. I'd like you to bundle them up, so I can take them to the dump with the rest of the trash. There's twine on the workbench. Doesn't need to be done right away, but don't wait too long. I don't want to have to go to the dump tomorrow. Your troop plays a game tomorrow, does it not?"

"Yes, sir," Red said. "And we got a better team now that Scooter's playing and Smokin' Joe Durkin helped us out."

"Well, we're all excited to see you fellas play. Now then, I think that's all. You two are excused. Don't forget to bundle the papers."

Scooter led Red to his bedroom and the treasure trove of baseball cards in the cigar boxes under his bed. They looked through them, one box at a time, laying some out for possible trades. But Scooter wasn't willing to give up a Lou Gehrig and a Roger Hornsby, which Red felt was a fair trade for his Babe Ruth. Scooter would have traded one of his several Ty Cobb, but Red had the same ones.

The boys almost settled on a Hack Wilson, a Dizzy Dean, and a Mickey Cochran (all bubble gum cards) and a Honus Wagner (a Piedmont cigarette card) for the Ruth card. But at the last minute, Red backed out. "Make that Wagner card a Gehrig and you got a deal," he said.

But Scooter wasn't willing to part with his only Gehrig, so they agreed to keep the trade talks open.

Play Ball!

Scooter put his cards away and grabbed his bat. They were down the driveway on their way to the Hollow when Scooter remembered the pile of newspapers.

"You go on ahead. I gotta tend to them newspapers in the garage. I'll catch up in a jiffy. Tell 'em I'm coming."

"Can't you do the papers later?"

"Best do the papers now," Scooter responded, not knowing when his grandfather wanted to go the dump.

"Can I take your bat? It's ever'body's favorite."

"Sure. But then I get dibs on mitts."

* * * * * *

There was quite a stack of newspapers. Scooter hadn't noticed such a mess in the corner of the garage before. He found the twine and laid a long strand of it on the floor. Then he began laying the papers neatly, one atop the other, on the twine until he had a stack. He gathered the ends of the twine and tied the papers into a bundle and carried it to the trunk of the Packard.

Scooter repeated the process and was on his third bundle when he discovered a strange mound under the stack. He nudged the mound carefully, hoping it wasn't a dead rat or something equally as disgusting. Instead his hand caught the edge of what seemed to be a leather purse or pouch. He pulled it out from under the mess of newspapers.

It was a baseball mitt! Slowly he turned it over. It was a Mel Ott Professional Model. An attached note read,

Doing good turns for others should be it's own reward. But aren't you glad you decided to do this one?

Mother, Father, and Grandfather Secory

The yelp of joy from Scooter's lips startled the chickens in their coop on the other side of the garage wall. His grandfather later claimed some didn't lay for two days. And Scooter's dance as he came out of the garage made the widow Bach think he had put his finger into a light bulb socket.

Truthfully, Scooter would have given up the eggs and stuck his finger in a light socket to hold his very own Mel Ott Professional Model baseball mitt. As he burst into the kitchen he found his mother and his grandfather standing there smiling. He forgot he was almost a grown boy and gave his mother a big hug.

"We knew how hard it was for you to leave our

other place and your school and your friends. And you did it without complaining. You were a real man about it. I'm so proud of you. We all wanted to make it up to you somehow. I hope you like it and it's what you wanted."

Scooter buried his face in his mother's apron hoping it would dry his eyes. Then he turned to his grandfather who was saying, "We're real proud of you, son. Now tomorrow, you can show them what a Secory's made of."

Scooter was so overcome he didn't know what to say. Then little Russell broke the silence. "How come Thcooter's cryin'?" and at that they all had a good laugh.

* * * * * *

Scooter's first day as a delivery boy went well. For the first hour he helped Mrs. Webber, the lady at the counter, fill orders. Customers came into the store with a list or told Mrs. Webber what they wanted and she and Scooter fetched the goods from the shelves. About four o'clock the phone rang with the first delivery order. From then on, Scooter was on the run. Mrs. Banning was first with an order of five pounds of sugar and a pound of pork chops. Then the minister's wife at the Dutch Reformed

Church ran out of flour in the middle of baking bread. Old lady Smitter needed a can of baking powder and a pound of ground beef. And so it went. By the time Scooter returned from delivering one order, there were one or two more waiting.

It was after six o'clock when Scooter finished what was supposed to be the last delivery of the day. "Did you make any deliveries before they hung up, Scooter?" jolly Mr. Cashmere wanted to know.

Scooter realized it was a joke. "I tried."

"Ha, Ha. You tried. Did you year that, Elsie? He tried. That's a good one..." he was interrupted by the ringing of the phone. "Don't go just yet, Scooter. This could be a delivery." It was. Doc Higgins' housekeeper, Mrs. Berg, needed a few things for their supper and time had gotten away from her. Was it too late for a delivery? Mr. Cashmere assured her it wasn't and Scooter waited for another sack of groceries to deliver.

"You tell Mrs. Berg I put something new in with her groceries. It's a package of frozen carrots. You tell her to try them and tell me how she likes them. It's sump'in new. Frozen foods. Wave of the future they tell me. You take care. Doc Higgins is a good customer, Scooter. I'd be surprised if there isn't a tip in this one for you."

Play Ball!

As he hurried along, Scooter wondered if he would encounter Doolie. He recalled his Grandfather's words, "When you look way down deep, Doolie's bluster is probably shallow." Look deep? It's shallow? Scooter smiled at his grandfather's humor and wisdom. But his smile faded quickly when he rang the bell at the Higgin's house and found himself face to face with Doolie.

"What do you want, kid?" Doolie snarled.

"Delivery for Mrs. Berg."

"And what if she's not here?"

Doolie's bluster didn't seem so shallow close up. Scooter's impulse was to drop the bag of groceries and run. But he remembered how Dutchie had successfully stood up to Doolie. "It's your supper, not mine."

"'Zat so?" At which point an older woman appeared behind Doolie.

"Oh, the delivery boy. Thanks for hurrying right over. Just a minute, let me get my purse. Lester, take the bag from the boy and put it on the kitchen counter."

Scooter snickered at Doolie when Mrs. Berg called him Lester.

Doolie narrowed his eyes and set his jaw as if to say, "Wipe that snicker off'n your face or I'll wipe it off for you." When he took a menacing step toward Scooter, Scooter also took a step toward Doolie. He held out the bag of groceries to the bully as if he thought it was Doolie's intention to reach for it. Doolie grabbed the bag if he were snatching something Scooter wanted to hold back from him. Then Mrs. Berg appeared behind him and held out a nickel. "That's for being so prompt, young man. You're new, aren't you? What's your name?

"Thank you, Ma'am," Scooter said as he took the nickel. "Gregory Secory. Ma'am, Mr. Cashmere put a package of frozen carrots in with your order. He'd like you to try 'em and tell him what you think. Supposed to be the thing of the future—frozen things."

"I don't know. . .are they safe? I never heard of such a thing. Frozen carrots. What will they think of next?" Then she turned her attention to Scooter. "Are you a friend of Lester's?"

"I play with Lester some. But we're not friends exactly. Thanks again, Ma'am. See you later, Lester." Scooter smiled at Doolie and turned quickly for home. No sense in going within the chain of a vicious dog. Besides, he couldn't wait to get the feel of the Mel Ott Professional Model baseball mitt that was waiting under his bed.

Play Ball!

* * * * * *

Saturday was born that morning with all the glory of a June day. No clouds and a gentle breeze that would keep it from getting muggy. The game was at ten o'clock, but Scooter was ready to go at eight-thirty. His father had shown him how to put linseed oil on his new mitt to keep the leather soft, and it had not left his hand except for breakfast when he put it under his chair.

At nine o'clock Grandfather had sent him on his way to the field by himself. . ."before you scare the chickens into a dither with your pacing about." The family would come later in the Packard. Scooter took off on a run and spotted Dutchie as he came around the corner of Howard.

"When you playing today?" Dutchie asked before he saw what Scooter was carrying. "Jeepers creepers! You get a new mitt? Can I see it?"

"My troop's playing at ten."

"So's mine. You playing for the Episcopalians? I didn't think, but that's where your grandpa goes, isn't it?"

"Yep. You on the Dutch Reformed team?"

"Yeh, can I have dibs on your mitt when you're batting?"

129

"Sure."

"C'mon, let's shake a leg."

As they passed Doc Higgins' house, Scooter was relieved that Doolie was nowhere in sight. He had pulled the bully's chain by deliberately calling him Lester. Scooter thought it was all well and good for his grandfather to suggest that the bully's bluster was shallow, but his grandfather wasn't in any danger of getting walloped.

* * * * * *

"Tommy Hammond will be our pitcher for the first three innings," the team members assembled around Coach Farley nodded their approval. "Gary Slatski will play first base and pitch the last three innings. David Berilla, play second base. Gregory Secory, shortstop. Red, you play third base, Michael Beck take left field, Benjamin Stone play center, and Woodrow Nelson go to right field. Theodore VanderVeen, you get the catcher's gear on."

As Scooter stood there listening to Coach Farley, he saw his family making their way through the crowd of parents sitting on the rise. His ma spread a blanket on the ground for herself and little Russell, but his grandfather stood up to watch.

"Now listen up, Scouts. If we all remember some

of the things Smokin' Joe told us and keep our head in the game, we can win this morning. So let's take the field and show 'em what Troop 23 is made of! Let's go!"

With a collective shout, they all took off for the positions Coach Farley had assigned them. A man with a blue suit came on the field and stood behind Hammy who began throwing his warm-up pitches to Coach Farley while Teddy VanderVeen got into the catcher's gear. When Teddy was ready the umpire called, "Play ball" and the biggest drama in Scooter's young life to date began.

His heart was pounding so loud Scooter was sure that barefooted Red, playing third base next to him, could hear it. He pounded his fist into the pocket of his Mel Ott Professional Model Mitt and watched Dutchie come to the plate as the first batter.

Dutchie jumped all over Hammy's first pitch and knocked a clean single over Chappy's head. Scooter didn't recognize the next batter, but his teammates were calling him Beans. Scooter remembered that Dutchie had told him that Beans Mulder played on his Scout team.

"C'mon, 23. Let's hear some chatter out of you!" Coach Farley shouted. Immediately a chorus of "Aay batta, batta. Aay batta, batta" came from the fielders.

Scooter chose instead to talk to Hammy. "C'moan key-ed. Fireitinthere nouw-ah!" It was a sing-song chatter he had heard when he watched Keller Tool play Story & Clark. They didn't say "Aay batta, batta" in Independent Ball.

"Where's the play, 23?" Coach Farley shouted the question.

"Second base!" came the responses somewhere among "aay" and "batta" and "batta."

Hammy's first pitch was a ball. The umpire called the second a strike. The third pitch was high, but the Mulder boy swung and hit a grounder to Scooter, who knocked it down, then scooped it up with his Mel Ott Professional Model Mitt. He had raced to second base and beat Dutchie by three steps when he heard the sweetest words in the English language to the ears of a fielder, "Yer' out at second!"

"Now where's the play 23?" Coach Farley shouted again.

"Second base," was the reply again and the chorus, made up mostly of boy sopranos, began their "aay, batta, batta."

Scooter changed his chatter a bit to something else he had heard at the Keller game. "C'moan key-ed, humithard!" He could only guess that "hum it hard" meant to throw the pitch hard, but he was sure it had to be neat to say if the Independent ballplayers said it.

The next batter struck out, and the next one walked, putting runners on first and second.

"We have a force out at any base, 23. Take the easiest one," Coach Farley advised.

The next batter hit a pop-up foul ball just off first base, which Slats caught easily. Troop 23 was up to bat. Scooter handed his new mitt to Dutchie as they passed on the field. "No catching my hits with this–I call," Scooter said with a grin.

"No hitting them at me, then," was the reply.

"Good catch, Gary," Coach Farley said as he patted Slats on the back. "And that's the way to stay with the play, Gregory. Now troop, let's get some runs. Tommy Hammond bats first, then Stone, then Slatski, Secory. . .," he went through the lineup.

"That's good," Slats said to Scooter who was swinging a bat in a wide arc over his head, first with one hand, then the other as he warmed up for his turn. "They got Dutchie pitchin'. We know we can hit off'n him."

"You get on and save me a rap," Scooter said.

Hammy was first up and was a left-handed hit-

Play Ball!

ter. "Lefty!" Dutchie called out to warn his team-mates. He waited for them to shift more to the right side of the infield and outfield to defend against the left-handed hitter. Now a chorus of "aay batta, batta" rose up from the other choir in the game.

"See the big space the third baseman leaves be-tween himself and the bag?" Slats whispered to Scooter. Scooter noticed and nodded. "Watch this," Slats said behind his hand.

Dutchie's first two pitches were called balls, and the third one looked like it was going to be outside for a ball. But it was the pitch Hammy was looking for. He stroked a sharp grounder down the third base line—fair ball—and the third baseman had no chance to make a play because he had shifted so far toward the right side of the infield. "You give Hammy the baseline like that, and he'll do that ever' time. Too bad it's only good for once a game. Next time up, they won't shift on him like that."

Stony struck out, bringing Slats up to the plate. He hit Dutchie's first pitch—a liner over the second baseman's head. Hammy made it all the way to third on the single to right field.

Scooter's turn! "C'mon Scooter," he heard his ma call out and then "C'mon Thcooter," little Russell squealed in excitement.

Scooter stepped into the batter's box and set his feet apart like Smokin' Joe had told him. He reached the bat out to tap the plate and looked at Dutchie who was grinning. There were no words, but there was communication. Scooter looked at Dutchie as if to say, *I dare you to bring it over the plate.*

Dutchie's looks said, *You couldn't hit this pitch if'n you tried.*

Amid the chorus of "aay batta, batta" from the field, the first pitch was a ball. The next pitch Scooter swung at and missed. He stepped out of the batter's box and took a couple of practice swings to get the feel of transferring his weight like Smokin' Joe had told him. Relax, he told himself, but he didn't listen.

What's the matter, you scared? was what the grin on Dutchie's face said. Scooter ignored him and stepped in to bat.

"Aay batta, batta. Aay batta, batta," the fielders' chatter was nonstop.

Dutchie's pitch was right down the middle, and Scooter watched it right into his swinging bat and launched it. It was a long line drive that got between the left and center fielders. It was a stand-up double that allowed both Hammy to score from third and Slats to come home all the way from first base. Scooter stood on second base like it was the top of the world. He squeezed his eyes shut and felt his heart pounding. It was as if he might explode with excitement.

Scooter snuck a peek at his grandfather. He was shaking both fists high in the air and grinning from ear to ear. Scooter couldn't hear his mother's shouts above the noise of his teammates.

Only Dutchie seemed to ignore the ruckus. He went about the business of striking the next batter out and getting the next batter to ground out to the first baseman. So Scooter was stranded on second base and the inning was over, but Troop 23 led 2 - 0.

* * * * * *

It was a great morning for Troop 23, winning 8 - 3. Coach Farley was ecstatic. "Great job, Scouts! Great job! That's the way to play baseball," he said as he patted backs and shook hands.

Scoutmaster McHenry was equally pleased and beamed. "If we can play that way next Saturday, I shouldn't wonder we may be in contention for the blue ribbons."

It was a really great morning for Scooter. He had gotten on base four times, with a walk, a single, a double, and once being safe on an error. His double scored two runs and his single with runners on second and third scored two more. All that made him feel good. But what made him feel even better was knowing that he—the new kid on the block—had found his place. He had become a part of something bigger than himself, and he had contributed to the success of that something.

Of course, hearing his grandfather offering to take the family to Mulder's Drug Store for ice cream cones to celebrate the victory didn't hurt his feelings either.

Chapter Ten

Big Doin's

"Sunday morning, Slugger. Get up. Gotta go to church. Breakfast is almost ready," his father's voice shattered Scooter's dreams right in the middle of making a delivery that was sure to fetch a nickel or dime tip. "C'mon, your mother's making blueberry pancakes and bacon. It's a ballplayer's breakfast."

"Mmmmph." Scooter rolled out and checked under the bed. They were all there: the bat, the Mel Ott Professional Model Mitt, and the cigar boxes with the baseball cards—still lacking a Babe Ruth. And he made his way toward the smell of bacon frying.

"Good morning, Scooter. I hope you could sleep after all the excitement of yesterday," Grandfather Secory was already at his place at the head of the table. "I'm not sure you and your fellow Scouts will be able to sit still in church this morning after that big victory. What do you think?"

"Gee willikers, Gramps. I slept like a log. I was tired."

"When do you play next?"

"Next Saturday. They have a tournament in the morning. Lot of the troops are playing. I ferget who exactly. But they are giving blue ribbons to the winners."

"Goodness, they're playing on the Fourth of July?" his mother asked as she brought platter of pancakes to the table. "Aren't you going to march in the parade?"

"There's bugs in my pan-a-cakes," little Russell exclaimed.

"Those aren't bugs, sweetie. Those are blueberries. I put them special in the pancakes, just for my big boys. Try 'em. You'll like 'em."

"I doesn't like bugs," replied Russell, not convinced.

"Just try one teensy bite. Look, Gregory's eating his. Papa's eating his."

"You better eat 'em if you want to grow up big and tall like your brother," Grandfather Secory urged.

"You eatin' the bugs, Thcooter?" little Russell was serious.

"They're good bugs, Maynard."

"I'n not Maynard," the little guy replied with a mischievous grin.

Big Doin's

"Don't you have to march in the parade?" His mother thought it best to steer the conversation away from the bugs in the pancakes.

"We gotta do that, too. Mr. McHenry said playing games doesn't mean we don't march. It's our responsibility to march. Games are just for fun. Please pass the syrup, Papa."

"So you're playing in the morning and marching in the afternoon. Will you be wearing your blue ribbons on your sashes?"

"We will if we win 'em."

* * * * * *

The Secorys took the Packard to the St. John's Episcopal Church. Scooter had on his good knickers and a white shirt and tie. His grandfather had made him polish his good shoes. "The first time you show up it's important to make a good impression," he had said. "So I think you should work at getting some of the scuffs outa those shoes, so's they don't look secondhand."

As they were ushered down the aisle, Scooter saw many of his teammates sitting with their families. The Berillas, the Stones, and the Hammonds were there. The Secorys were ushered to a pew across the aisle from Red Van Dorn and his family.

140

Scooter snuck a look at Red's feet. He had shoes on.

There was a time for announcements and the pastor expressed the sympathy of the congregation to the DeBoer family on the loss of Marvin DeBoer in a tragic accident at the sawmill. He also announced a need for contributions of food for their pantry for there were many needy families in the community. He indicated there was also a need for some additional volunteers to help with the soup kitchen on Wednesdays and Fridays.

Then he paused and looked out over the congregation. "I'm also pleased to announce that our Scout Troop 23 posted their second victory of the season in a win over the troop from First Reformed. Congratulations to Scoutmaster McHenry and Coach Farley and all the boys."

After the service it was Scoutmaster McHenry who observed that the members of the troop had been particularly attentive in the service that morning. Merrill Secory wondered out loud if they were listening to the sermon or replaying the baseball game of the morning before. Then the conversation turned more serious.

"Too bad about Marv DeBoer."

"Such a tragedy. He was so young."

Big Doin's

"Leaving two small children as well as a widow. It's so sad."

"You can't be too careful, working in a sawmill."

Slats was standing next to Scooter as the menfolk talked. "You know who they're talkin' about, don't you?"

Scooter shook his head.

"That's Casey's uncle who died."

"Casey goes to this church, too?"

"I think the whole DeBoer family does. They're usually here. Probably didn't come because of what happened."

After church, the Secory's packed a picnic lunch and spent the day at the beach. They swam in the breakers of Lake Michigan, ate chicken salad and egg salad sandwiches and drank lots of lemonade. They watched men catching perch off the pier that guarded the harbor, played catch, and swam some more. When everyone began showing sunburns, they packed up their gear, loaded it back into the Packard, and headed for home.

* * * * * *

There weren't enough players for teams on Monday morning, but with ten kids, it was a great game. To Scooter's relief, Doolie didn't show up. With that many players, they could play first base was out instead of pitcher's hands, and there could be three batters, so no automatic second. That favored the good hitters. Along toward the noon whistle, Scooter was up with Slats and Casey. The three of them were among the best hitters that morning, and the fielders were struggling to get any of them out. Slats had just hit a double to knock Casey in from second base. As Scooter came up to bat, Casey suddenly announced to Scooter that he had to go home.

"How come?" Scooter asked.

Casey looked embarrassed. "'Cuz I have to go to the bathroom," he said quietly.

"Just go in the bushes over there."

"I can't."

"Why not. Ever'body else does."

"Just 'cuz I can't. I have to go home." And with that, Casey took off on a run.

"Casey had to go home early, so ever' body move up. Want to go to two outfielders or pitcher's hands is out?"

"Pitcher's hands" were the responses.

They played on until the noon whistle.

* * * * * *

There was a last minute delivery that afternoon,

so Scooter didn't get home until six-thirty and his family was waiting for him for dinner.

"I made them wait, Gregory," his mother said. "We're having spaghetti with meatballs, one of your favorites. I was afraid if I let them start without you, there'd be nothing left for my working man. So now that you're here, we can eat. Did you wash your hands, sweetie?"

It was a steaming bowl of spaghetti and a large bowl of red sauce with meatballs mounding up in it. Grandfather Secory said grace and they dug in. Peter Secory told how one of the boats needed new fuel injectors. Since none were available for several weeks out of Detroit, he had made them from scratch. They weren't as good as new, but they would last until proper ones could be ordered. Lawrence Dornbos had been pleased. "You're the best, Peter. Don't know what I'd do without you," he had said.

Merrill Secory was very pleased to hear Dornbos's compliment.

Scooter told about a delivery at the Deurs. When he came through their front gate a big boxer had come bounding around the side of the house barking like to scare the devil himself. "I thought to drop the groceries and run, but there were both eggs and bread and I remembered how you told me not to drop the eggs, Gramps."

"Goodness sakes, so what did you do," his mother was concerned.

"Just before the dog nearly killed me, old lady Deur came out of the house and screamed at the dog in Dutch, and he went from barking at me to licking me."

"So everything turned out okay?"

"Like I said, I didn't drop the eggs, but just before I thought the dog was going to kill me, I think I squeezed the bread."

Everyone laughed.

"So you didn't get killed, but you took a licking?" Grandfather asked with a twinkle in his eyes.

"With the size of that boxer's tongue and him pawin' on me, I think it might have been better to be killt and been done with it."

"Did Mrs. Deur tip you after that?" Scooter's mother wanted to know.

"I can answer that," the old man interjected. "Most assuredly she did not. There's a woman could fertilize her garden with what she can squeeze out of a nickel."

His grandfather was right, there was no tip. But fertilize her garden with a nickel?

His father saw the question on Scooter's face. "What he means is that if you squeeze the buffalo on a nickel hard enough, the buffalo will poop and you'll get fertilizer for your garden. It's a way of saying Mrs. Deur was tight with a nickel–very, very frugal."

The image of old Mrs. Deur squeezing a nickel over her garden to get the buffalo to provide fertilizer got Scooter to giggling. Then his mother started, and they couldn't stop. Soon the whole table was laughing.

"Well, Doc Higgins says that laughter is good for the digestion, so I expect after that laugh we all should have room for dessert. Did I see you making a cherry pie, Ruthie?"

"Can't keep any secrets from you, can I? Who'll have a piece?"

All the hands went up.

"You want cherry pie, too, Russell?" Grandfather Secory asked. "You sure you got room for pie? You ate an awful belly full of spaghetti."

"My likes cherry pie," Little Russell said with a devilish look in his eye. "It's good junk, Maynard," he added and everybody laughed.

"Good. Scooter, will you clear the dishes while I cut the pie?"

Big Doin's

The Secory family were savoring the pie, mouthful by delicious mouthful when Grandfather said, "Did you see the paper this afternoon, Peter?"

"No, I got home late and haven't had a chance. What's in it."

"Remember back in February some time, when that new leader of Germany, Adolph Hitler broke his promise to Neville Chamberlain and had his army reclaim the Rhineland. I said at the time he was trouble. Well, in the paper tonight, there's a story that he's mounting a campaign against Jewish people, mostly bankers and financers and the like. Says they were the cause of Germany's troubles after the War. Some mighty influential people in the finance ministry and the big banks have been told they're no longer welcome and they are looking to get out of Germany. I still say this Hitler fella's trouble, and I'm glad we got some water between him and us.

"Then," the old man paused if he were trying to remember the second thing he had read in the paper that evening. "Oh, yes. I saw a big advertisement for doin's over to Ferry Field," the old man said in an exaggerated voice. Scooter had heard that tone of voice before. This wasn't conversation like the story about Hitler. This was an announcement.

Scooter decided to play along. He knew from the handbill what the big doings were— the All-Stars playing the Pittsburgh Crawfords.

"Really, Gramps? What sort of big doin's could be goin' on at Ferry Field?"

"Oh, these big doin's are for grown-ups. I don't think they're for kids. I don't think kids would care for these doin's a'tall."

"Really, Pops? Am I the only one who doesn't know what's going on at Ferry Field?" Peter asked, sensing that Scooter had already figured out what was up.

"I doesn't know," little Russell chimed in.

"Neither do I," said Ruthie. "Tell us, what's the big doin's."

"The Pittsburgh Crawfords are coming to town to play the local All-Stars," Scooter replied.

"Who are the Pittsburgh Crawfords, if I may ask," inquired Scooter's mother.

Scooter was ready with the answer. "They're the Negro National League baseball champions, and they're going to play All-Stars from the Independent League come Friday."

"I'd really like to see that," the old man ventured. "How about you, Peter?"

"Sounds good to me. I'll bet it costs a fortune to

get in, though. We probably couldn't afford to take everybody, could we?" Peter Secory was now the one with the exaggerated voice. He had learned how to play his father's games very well.

"The handbill I read said that kids are free," Scooter said.

"Kids are free?" his grandfather said in mock surprise. "I didn't see that in the ad. Are you sure? Let me get the paper and check that out." And he left the table as if he didn't know and really needed to check it out. For a moment, Scooter had a doubt. Maybe they changed the rules or didn't have it in the paper that kids were free.

"Let's see, the ad's right here," the old man said as he came back into the kitchen with the paper open. "Sez right here. Admission fifty cents. By golly, you're right, Scooter. Kids free when accompanied by an adult. Do you know any adults who'll take you?"

"I was hoping we could take Red and Dutchie, too. I don't think their pas will be going."

"I don't see any reason not to. What do you say, Peter? Want to go see a ball game with an old man and a couple' a young whippersnappers?"

Big Doin's

* * * * * *

The days slipped by. Every night Scooter had a story to tell about his delivery job. Mrs. Bryson asked him to get her cat out of the tree, which was good for some real deep scratches on his arms and a nickel tip. Mrs. Bryson had insisted she treat the scratches with iodine, which hurt worse than the scratches and made his arm all red.

Thursday night was baseball practice and Coach Farley had tried Scooter out as pitcher.

"How did you do?" his father asked when he got home from practice. The family was sitting around the kitchen table having cookies and coffee or milk.

"I'm prolly as good as Hammy, but Slats is better than me. I can throw harder, but he throws more strikes."

"Is the team ready for the big tournament on Saturday," Scooter's mother wanted to know.

"All except Woody. He's not the best. He doesn't hit well, and I think Coach Farley puts him in right field to hide him."

"Hide him? He's out in right field in plain view of everybody," she said.

"What he means, Ruthie, is that fewer balls are hit to right field, so you put your worst fielder there where he can do the least damage to the team,"

Grandfather Secory explained.

"That's not very nice. Does Woodrow know he's hiding."

"He's not hiding; he's being hid. He knows he shouldn't play in the infield. If he plays in the infield and makes a lot of mistakes where everybody sees it, he'd really feel bad. Better to feel a little bit bad where no one knows you're feeling bad." Scooter's logic was hard to argue with, so no one at the table tried.

"Do you know which team you play on Saturday?" his grandfather wanted to know.

"Troop 24. It's the team Doolie and Bub Denton play on. Dutchie says they're the best team this year."

"Have you asked Donny and Red if they would like to go to see the All-Stars play the Crawfords?" his father asked.

"Sure. They're real excited about going. Can we go early so's we can get on the sand box and chase foul balls?"

"Maybe I should pick you up at Cashmere's at six. We should plan on a light supper so we can be sure to get there on time. I'd like to get a good seat, too. I hear some of these Negro fellas are's good as a lot of Major League players. Can you get your friends over here by 6:30?"

* * * * * *

The game between the All-Stars and the Pittsburgh Crawfords was 'big doin's.' There were a lot of cars and bicycles parked on the streets around Ferry Field when the Packard pulled up at 6:45 that Friday evening. Near the entrance to the field was a large yellow bus with "Pittsburgh Crawfords" painted on its side.

Scooter's grandfather paid the dollar admission and once they were inside, the boys broke into a dead run for the sand box. It was empty and they climbed atop it. The Crawfords were in the dugout along the left foul line. Their pitchers and catchers were warming up near the sand box. The boys had a program with pictures of the Negro players and began identifying them by their pictures. Satchel Paige was warming up with Josh Gibson so close, the boys could hear them breathe. Next to them Fireball Smith was throwing to a catcher they couldn't identify. There was Cool Papa Bell and Judy Johnson, all big powerful men.

"From the sound Satchel Paige's pitches are makin' when they smack into Gibson's glove, the All-Stars are in for some kind of trouble," was

Dutchie's prediction.

"I didn't know a fella could throw that hard," Scooter said. "You can hardly see it. How can you get your bat around in time to hit those pitches?"

"I'd have to start swinging before he threw the ball," Red said and the others agreed.

"Get of'n that sand box, you little creeps. Bub and I are gonna sit there." It was Doolie Higgins! And when he saw Scooter, he snarled, "And I've got a score to settle with you, smarty-pants-delivery-boy."

"We were here first, Doolie," Dutchie was quick to defend their seats.

"I said get of'n that sand box, or do I have to knock you off? And I reckon I'll start with the smart-ass-delivery-boy." Doolie moved toward them all but looked directly at Scooter.

"What'cha gonna do, start a fight in front of all these people? Still working on your merit badges for bullyin' and cussin'? Why don't you go sit with your pa like a good boy?"

Doolie's eyes narrowed, and he looked around. The folks who were sitting in the stands near the sand box were all watching. Satchel Paige had stopped warming up, and Josh Gibson was looking at the scene as well. This was not the time or place for a scene. Besides he had come with his father who would surely hear any ruckus.

"Come on, Denton, we'll sit somewheres else. But I ain't finished with you creeps. 'Specially you, smarty-pants-delivery-boy!"

After Doolie and Bub went to find other seats, Dutchie turned to Scooter. "What'd you do to set him off like that?"

"I called him Lester when I made a delivery to his house."

"You're either brave or stupid. Either which way, that wasn't too smart. But use the merit badge thing about bullyin' if'n he ever really comes to lay a whuppin' on you."

"My grandpa doesn't think bullies will fight if you stand up to them. He says way down deep, they're really shallow."

"Yeh, but your grandpa doesn't have to fight 'em."

* * * * * *

The game got underway after the High School Band played the "Star-Spangled Banner." Then the announcer gave the names of the players over a loudspeaker system that no one could understand. The Crawfords, as the visiting team, batted first.

Big Doin's

Smokin' Joe Durkin was the starting pitcher for the All-Stars. He walked the first batter on four pitches, then took his time before he started pitching to the second batter. Settling his nerves, Scooter thought. Durkin fingered the rosin bag and kicked some dirt away from the pitching rubber. When he was ready, Jimmy Critchfield was the batter. Smokin' Joe was determined to get his first pitch to Critchfield over the plate, and Critchfield seemed to sense that. He drove the pitch off the left field wall. It was then that the superiority of the Negro team started to become evident. The speed of the runner who had walked was so great, he seemed to fly around the bases and was able to score easily all the way from first base.

The next batter was the legendary catcher, Josh Gibson. He hit Smokin' Joe's first pitch so far over the center field fence it landed on Griffin Street and lit on Mr. Pool's front porch on the second bounce.

"Holy cow!," Dutchie said. "Nobody's ever hit a ball that far before. Nobody!"

When the commotion from the towering home run died down, the next batter bunted safely. He attempted to steal second when the next batter smacked a line drive right at the shortstop. A quick throw to first base doubled off the runner who couldn't get back to the bag in time. The next batter hit a long fly ball to left field that the All-Star's left fielder made a nice running catch on, ending the inning for the Crawfords.

The All-Stars were very good baseball players. And all who watched this game were soon aware of the big difference between the Major Leagues and amateur baseball. While none of the Pittsburgh Crawfords ever played in the Major Leagues, some of them were every bit as good as many of the white men who did play in the Major Leagues. Players like Satchel Paige, Josh Gibson, Judy Johnson, and Cool Papa Bell were among the best in the game, and only the color of their skin kept them from appearing on the baseball cards in the cigar boxes under Scooter's bed.

As the game went on, the All-Stars saw pitches from Satchel Paige like none they'd never seen before. He would go through his famous windup, and then hesitate like he didn't know what pitch he was throwing. There would be blazing fastballs. Or the pitch might be a curve ball that seemed to come at the batter's head and then dive down over the plate. He might pitch another fastball, then go through his famous windup and deliver a pitch that seemed to float to the plate.

An All-Star's batter, Steve Saluka, managed to get his bat on one of Paige's floaters and send a high foul pop-up down the third base line. It drifted toward the sand box and sent the three friends scurrying. Scooter misjudged the edge of the box and tumbled off–landing flat on his back and staring up at the fly ball that was now coming down straight toward him and the box.

The Crawfords' third baseman, Judy Johnson, had made his way over to the sand box and called, "Got her, got her." He reached out over the box and neatly caught the pop-up, holding the ball up for all to see. He then looked down at Scooter, who was still lying flat on his back looking up at the big black man in the pin-stripped uniform.

"You okay, boy?" Johnson asked.

"Yes, Sir. I just fell."

And at that, Johnson flipped the ball to Scooter. "Keep it, boy. Ain't no shame in fallin'. Only shame's not gettin' up each and ever' time."

Chapter Eleven

Fourth of July Fireworks

The sound of cherry bombs and M-80s exploding in the neighborhood woke Scooter, reminding him that it was the Fourth of July. When he had brushed away the cobwebs of sleep, he reached under his pillow and found the ball Judy Johnson had given him right where he had put it the night before. It was a beauty; pure white leather with bright red stitching so tight, it seemed like the cover would never come off. It was another treasure for the growing trove under Scooter's bed.

"How come the Negroes can't play in the Majors, Gramps," Scooter asked between bites of scrambled eggs.

"They can, can meaning 'able.' They mayn't. They aren't allowed to because they're Negroes. The baseball owners won't hire black men on their teams."

"Why not? Don't they want the best players to help their teams win?"

"Well, yes. But a lot of people don't want to mingle with Negroes, eat in the same places with them, sleep in the same beds they slept in. So they try to keep them separate. It would be hard to have a Negro on a ball team because of those feelings that a lot of people have."

"Why would it be hard?"

"Because there are a lot of hotels and restaurants that won't allow Negroes. They couldn't even travel with the team."

"Just because they're black?"

"Well, black makes them seem different. And it's the difference that makes folks feel that way. There was a time when the railroad wouldn't hire Irish Catholics. But eventually the Irish people proved themselves to be. . .well, just people like everybody else. So they finally got hired on the railroad. One of my engineers was a great old Irishman name of O'Riley."

"Oh, really?"

"No, O'Riley."

"Gramps. . .," Scooter rolled his eyes at the old man's joke. Then he persisted. "But the Negroes have proven themselves. Dutchie said that nobody ever hit a ball farther than Josh Gibson."

"True enough, Don Badcon, the sports writer for the *Tribune* said as much last night. And Satchel Paige didn't allow but one hit in the whole game.

But as good as some of the Crawfords are, they're still Negroes and until folks change their attitudes, they won't play in the Major Leagues."

"I'm glad we don't see any of that around here," Ruthie's mother said.

"Don't paint your face black and try to get an ice cream cone at Mulder's Drug Store, m'dear," the old man said as he buttered another piece of toast.

"Surely you're not serious?" Scooter's mother was surprised.

"Mulder won't kick you out the door, but they'll be too busy to serve you even if you're the only one in the store."

"That ain't fair," Scooter said.

"Life isn't fair," the old man said with a sad note in his voice. "And life isn't gonna be fair. There are goin' to be times when someone thinks you're too young, other times when you'll be too old. Times when you wish you were a man, others when you wish you were a woman. And all the time, you have to play the cards dealt you. Being successful and happy isn't about getting a good hand, it's about playing the cards you're dealt the best you can.

"Take Satchel Paige, for example. Would he like to play in the Majors? I'm sure he would. But he's not sitting around pouting. He's risen to be the best he can be and do the best he can with what he's got. That's all any of us can do.

"Now speaking of doing the best we can. . .when is your baseball game this morning?"

"Eleven a'clock."

"Well, we got time to tend to the chickens and then you best get over there. We'll come along in time for the game."

"SCOOTER." Someone calling at the back door interrupted the old man.

Scooter recognized the voice. "Dutchie," he said. "Can I be excused?"

It was Dutchie. "I came to see if'n I could borrow your mitt, seein' as I play before you."

"S'okay. I'll get it."

* * * * * *

The scoreboard in right field told Scooter that Dutchie's game was in the third inning and one of the teams was ahead 16-5 when he got to Seventh Street Field. The field itself was a sight. There was red, white, and blue bunting on the backstop. The various scout troops had their flags and colors displayed. The grass was just mowed and new chalk lines had been put down. A lot of people were sitting on blankets on the rise. There were some older boys setting off firecrackers in a lot across the street. Miller's Dairy had two horse-drawn delivery wagons along the street, and there was a line of folks getting the free cold lemonade. The horses stomped at the sound of firecrackers.

Scooter spotted Slats and Casey sitting on the rise with some other kids and made his way through the crowd to them. "Who's winning?" he asked when he got to Slats and Casey.

"Dutchie's team is killin' 'em," Casey responded. "Dutchie got a triple with the bases loaded and then Beans homered. It's a slaughter. Do you know you play Doolie's team?"

"Yeh. They killt us the time we played them before, didn't they?" Scooter asked.

Slats nodded. "It wasn't pretty and Doolie was mockin' us the whole time. Especially Woody. I don't know why he has it in for Woody. But I hope to see the day Woody grows up bigger'n Doolie, walks up to him and says, 'Lester, you're a loser' and then knocks his block off." They all nodded in agreement. Although Scooter felt safe in the crowd, he looked around for Doolie, who was not to be found.

As they watched, the other team scored some runs to keep from getting mercied, but before long the game was over, with Dutchie's team winning 16 - 9. Slats and Scooter left Casey and the other kids and made their way through the people and blankets to the field.

"Doesn't Casey go to our church," Scooter asked Slats.

"Yah."

"How come he doesn't join the Scouts and play on our team? He's as good as you and me and better than most of the others."

Slats had stopped walking, and Scooter looked back to see why.

Slats was just standing there with his mouth open and a dumbfounded look on his face. "You kiddin'?"

"No. He'd be a heck of a lot better hitter than most, and he can pitch besides. How come he doesn't play. Won't his folks let him?"

"You ain't kidding, are you?"

"'Course I'm not kidding."

Suddenly Slats understood. "You don't know Casey's real name do you?"

"All's I know is 'Casey.' What's his name got to do with it?"

"His name is Cassandra, as in Cassandra Lynnae DeBoer. Casey can't join the Scouts because he's a girl."

"You're fun'un me," Scooter protested. "He can't be a girl. He's too good to be a girl. Ain't no girl I ever seen who can play baseball like that!"

Slats just stood there grinning. "She's been as good as any boy since we were old enough to be playing ball on the playground at school. What's the matter, you gonna be sick?"

Just then Dutchie came up to return Scooter's mitt. "Thanks for the loan of your mitt. I left some catches in it for you. What's the matter with you? You look like you're gonna puke or somethin'."

"He didn't know Casey was a girl," Slats offered.

"You didn't? Geez!" Dutchie was astonished. "She's always been a girl." Then he realized how funny that sounded. "I mean, she didn't just change."

Scooter wasn't feeling so good. "Couple'a days ago, he. . .Casey that is, said he had to go home because he, er she, had to go to the bathroom. I told her to go in the bushes like the rest of us do. Gee willikers. Now I know why he looked at me so funny."

"Why <u>she</u> looked at you so funny. What's the big deal? Just tell her you thought she was a boy."

"Oh sure, Slats. That would be sweet music to

any girl's ears. 'Sorry girlie, I thought you were a boy.'"

"Don't forget to say you're sorry for tellin' her to pee in the bushes in front of all of us."

"Oh yeh. I'm sorry for that too, girlie. Geeeeeeee willikers," Scooter moaned.

"Glad I'm not you. C'mon. Get your mind off'n girls. We got a game to play."

* * * * * *

"Okay, Scouts!" Coach Farley was rallying his players. "We'll go with the same lineup as we did last week. It won't be as easy this time. Troop 24 has but one loss. They're a tough team and they beat us before. But if we keep our heads in the game and do our best, I think we can beat them. Some of their players are bigger than some of us. But remember, the bigger they are the harder they fall."

"Or, as I like to say," Scoutmaster McHenry interjected, "It's not the size of the dog in the fight, it's the size of the fight in the dog."

"Yes. Well, we're the visitors," Coach Farley continued, "so we'll be batting first. I've decided on the same batting order as last week." He paused to look at his clipboard. "Tommy Hammond bats first, then Stone, then Slatski, Secory, VanderVeen. . .." He went through the lineup.

"Good. They got Bub Denton pitching," Slats said to Scooter as he was swinging a bat to warm up. "Usually they go with Doolie first. They think we're gonna be a pushover, so they can save Doolie for the end. 'Course it doesn't hurt them to have Doolie at shortstop like he is."

It also didn't hurt that there was a baseball field between Doolie Higgins and a certain grocery delivery boy with whom Doolie had a score to settle.

"Let's play ball," the umpire called out.

"Look, we got an ump behind the plate and one on the bases," Scooter said.

"They do that for the final championship game, too," Slats replied. Then he lowered his voice. "Look! They're giving Hammy the line."

Sure enough, after the pitcher had yelled "Lefty!," the third baseman had moved toward Doolie at short. Doolie was waving him back, but the third baseman paid him no mind or didn't hear him. He was shouting "Aay, batta, batta" at the top of his lungs.

Bub's first pitch was just where Hammy wanted it, and he stroked the ball down the third base line. It was a slow grounder that neither the pitcher or the third baseman could field on time, and Hammy was on first.

"The kid'll do it to you ever time," Slats said to Scooter. Then he turned to Stony "C'mon, Stony, rip it now-ah!"

Stony let Bub's first pitch go by, but it was called a strike. The second pitch was high. Stony swung and missed the third pitch, but connected with the next one and hit a grounder to the third baseman. He bobbled it momentarily, looked to throw to second but saw it would be too late. He then turned and threw the ball to first. But the throw was off the mark, and the ball got by the first baseman and went into the crowd. The umpire motioned to the runners to advance one base on the overthrow. Troop 23 had runners on second and third with nobody out. The crowd cheered wildly and Scooter picked out his family—his mother and Little Russell on a blanket; his father and grandfather standing nearby.

"You can hit this guy, Slats. A hit's two runs," Scooter urged and picked up his bat and started swinging it in wide arcs over his head—first with one arm then the other. He had watched Josh Gibson warm up in that fashion just the night before.

The "aay, batta, battas" began again as Slats

stepped up to the plate. But "aay battas" didn't bother Slats. He connected with Bub's second pitch for a double down the third baseline scoring Hammy and Stony with ease. Troop 23 was ecstatic, jumping up and down and yelling "Atta boy" and "Way to hit 'em, Slats." They were ahead 2 - 0 with nobody out and Scooter was up to bat.

Doolie Higgins signaled "time out" to the base umpire and trotted to the pitcher's mound.

"Time out," the base ump called raising both his arms in the air.

Scooter couldn't hear what Doolie was saying and had no idea what they were planning. Then he heard Casey calling from the rise. "C'mon, Scooter. You can hit him." He glanced over her way and caught her eye. She raised both arms with clenched fists."Take 'em to the fence," she hollered, and Scooter grinned and nodded.

We'll see if you're so friendly when you find out I thought you were a boy, Scooter thought.

"Play ball," the umpire called as Doolie returned to shortstop.

Scooter didn't get a chance to "take it to the fence," as Bub delivered four straight balls and walked him. "So that's what Doolie had up his sleeve—to walk me."

"That's okay, Gregory," Coach Farley said when Scooter reached first. "A walk's as good as a hit. Now if Teddy gets a hit, I want you to try to make it to third if you can. Take a good lead off on every pitch. Remember, there's nobody out."

What happened next Scooter couldn't remember, but enough people told him about it so he could form a clear picture of what transpired. He took a lead off with each pitch, like Coach Farley had instructed. On the third pitch Teddy VanderVeen hit a line shot that looked like it would be a clean single up the middle. But Doolie raced to his left with the crack of the bat, diving full out and making an impossible catch of the line drive. Doolie actually landed on second base when he fell, doubling off Slats for the second out.

Scooter, who apparently saw Doolie catch the line drive and fall, skidded to a stop and raced back toward first base to avoid being doubled off as well as making the third out—a triple play for Troop 24. Doolie jumped to his feet and threw the ball as hard as he could to make the force on Scooter at first base.

Scooter did remember wondering why the first baseman held his mitt out in such a way as to catch his head instead of the ball as he came back toward first base. Then there was a loud crash inside the back of his head. There were fireworks in his brain like shooting stars on the Fourth of July. He couldn't make his legs move properly, and then the lights went out. All of them.

Chapter Twelve

Doolie Higgins

There was something about that play that caused the crowd to focus on what was happening and to be quiet enough at the time so that no one forgot the sight of the ball hitting the back of Scooter's head or the sickening sound it made. Neither did they forget the scream that began in Ruth Secory's soul and found its expression in her throat.

It was almost as if the whole event happened in slow motion. *The ball moving on a direct line with Scooter's head. . .a terrible cracking, thudding sound at the moment of impact. . .the boy's head snapping forward from the force of the blow. . .his legs splaying out from under him as his hands went up as if to swat away a pesky fly. . .his body pitching forward toward the first baseman. . .the first baseman lurching to the side to avoid the stumbling, pitching body. . .Scooter falling face first into the dirt, his body flopping or rebounding up once. . .his arms and legs jerking convulsively just before his body became motionless. . .Ruth Secory's scream.* Then the slow motion stopped, and there was pandemonium.

The first person to reach Scooter was Coach Farley who saw the blood seeping from a very nasty spider-like wound that had opened where the ball struck. Next was the base umpire who, as it happened, was a medical corpsman in The War. He had ripped off his white cotton shirt as he ran up. He gently rolled Scooter over on his side to get his face out of the dirt and laid his shirt under his head to keep dirt out of the wound. The shirt was almost immediately soaked in blood, so he used his left hand to apply pressure to the wound with the shirt. Then he felt for a pulse at the base of Scooter's neck with his right. All of this took only a matter of seconds.

Scooter's mother was next. In her anxiety, she was of little help. "Oohh, how is he? Oohh, is he breathing? Oohh, somebody do something for my boy."

Peter Secory was right behind his wife and was followed closely by his father.

By this time, the Scouts from Troop 23 and some from Troop 24 were gathering around. "Make room, give the boy some air," Coach Farley directed.

Scooter's mother knelt in the dirt and held her son's hand. He had been transformed from a strong, athletic boy into a limp, lifeless-looking figure in matter of seconds, and there was nothing she could do now to prevent it or help it. Her tears fell and made jagged dots on the stone dust of the field.

"His pulse is strong but racing. He has a nasty wound where the ball hit him. He's unconscious. We best get him seen by a doctor right away. Did you come in your car, Merrill?" The umpire-turned-medic addressed his comments to Peter Secory, his question to the grandfather.

"I'll bring the car around to the top of the hill here if some of you fellas can help Peter get him up to the street." The grandfather was all concern and business as he hurried off to get the car.

"Help me get him up to my shoulder." Together the men lifted Scooter upright and his father got under him, draping him over his shoulder. The umpire-turned-medic held his blood-soaked shirt against the wound and they made off up the hill to the street. People picked up their blankets to make a path and then edged close to get a look. The sight of the blood-soaked shirt and the dangling arms and legs sent prayers heavenward–some for Scooter's recovery–some in gratitude it wasn't their son being trundled off the field like a large rag doll looking more dead than alive.

As Peter Secory manipulated himself and his load into the car, Scooter moaned and began to quiver. "He's coming around. That's a good sign," the medic said, trying to be encouraging to the concerned parents. He climbed into the back seat and re-applied the shirt to the wound. "I think the bleeding has slowed some," he said.

With Peter, Scooter, and the medic tucked into the back seat with the help of Mr. Farley, Ruthie got into the front seat, and Merrill Secory eased the Packard away from the curb. "Should we take him home or to the doctor's house?" he asked the medic or anyone else who had an opinion.

"I'd take him home and get him comfortable and then call for the doctor. It might be important not to handle him any more than necessary. Head injuries. . ." the medic checked himself and instead of saying ". . .can be fatal if you're not careful," finished his sentence with ". . .are not something to be moving about with." At the sound of the words "head injuries" and the pause, Ruth Secory lost her composure and began crying again. "I'd like him home," she said through her tears, which settled the matter.

It took only a few minutes to cover the three blocks to home, and as they pulled into the driveway, the medic spoke again. "He's moving about a bit. I'd keep him here in the car until everything is ready in the house. Then bring him in. Otherwise we will be jostling him about getting things situated."

"Okay, why don't you go in the house with Ruth and help her arrange things and then we'll bring him in. I'm okay with him here for a bit longer," Peter responded.

Once in the house, Ruth Secory took charge. "Father Secory, will you please ring up the doctor?" she said as she tied on her apron. Then she turned to the medic. "Where shall we put him and what will we need?"

"I'd put him in his bedroom. If you have a rubber sheet, I'd put that on his mattress and a sheet over that. There's likely to be some mess created by Doc cleaning him up and such. Doc will also want plenty of hot water and clean towels, preferably white."

When the bed was ready and Doc Higgins had been called, they went to get Scooter out of the car.

"He's just asked if Hammy and Stony scored. He's in sort of a twilight zone. He doesn't know what hit him or that he's been hit, just that his head hurts something awful. Is that good or bad?" Peter asked when the others got to the car.

"I don't rightly know, except that the sooner they come to and start asking questions, the better. Here, let us help you get him out of the car and into the house," the medic instructed.

Getting a 95-pound unconscious boy with dangling legs and arms out of the car and up the stairs was a tough job. But with the help of the stair railing and the medic, Peter Secory had his son in bed by the time the front door bell announced the arrival of the doctor.

Merrill went down to open the door.

"Well, Merrill, what do we have?" the doctor asked as Merrill took his hat and ushered him to the stairs.

"The boy took a baseball to the back of the head. Knocked him out colder than a mackerel. He's come around some, but he has a nasty gash on his noggin."

"Well, let's have a look at him," and he followed Merrill up the stairs. "What's the lad's name?"

"I think calling him Scooter would be some comfort to him. If you called him Gregory, he might think he's passed on and all, might give him a fright. He's in his room here."

"Well, well, Scooter is it? Let's have a look at

you. Do you know what happened to you?"

"I think I was on first base and. . ." his voice trailed off and the first tears started to form.

The doctor looked up to confirm what the boy had said only to be greeted with shaking heads.

"I see. Tell me, Scooter, does the back of your head hurt?"

"Yes."

"How about the front here?"

"All over."

"Well, I want you to close your eyes and keep them closed for a minute. I'm going to strike a match and when I tell you to, open your left eye. You know which eye is your left eye? Good." The doctor struck the match and held it close to Scooter's left eye. "Okay, I want you to open your left eye and keep it open and look at the match. Good. Now open your other eye. Good.

"Now, stay on your side. I'm going to have to clean up the back of your head and patch you up, young man. I've a feeling the baseball world needs you."

* * * * * *

The adults followed the doctor down to the living room. Scooter's parents held on to each other.

The medic stood in the background. Merrill got the doctor's hat.

"Well, as you know, he took a pretty good blow to the back of his head. He has a concussion and a possible skull fracture. The bone is not displaced, that is, out of place. But before I put those sutures in, I lifted up enough skin to see there is evidence of a possible fracture. There is no evidence of bleeding in the brain, which is a very good sign. He has amnesia about the incident, which is quite normal. We should expect some headaches and some disorientation for a few hours, maybe a day. Change the dressing twice a day until you can see the scab is hard. Use the ointment I left generously. It will prevent an infection. I recommend bed rest for twenty-four hours, then have him take it easy for a day or two. No baseball. His head will tell him when he's overdoing things a bit. But I expect he'll be back to normal long before the hair I shaved off grows back. I'll check back in the morning about ten o'clock.

"Oh, and one more thing," the doctor said as he reached for his hat and headed for the front door. He stopped and turned back toward them. "The best thing you can do is to teach him how to duck."

Doolie Higgins

Band music coming from the Fourth of July parade only two blocks away drifted in and out of Scooter's consciousness. He tried to march behind Scoutmaster George Ryan McHenry and Assistant Scoutmaster Roger Farley. *Too tired. . .head hurts,* Scooter tried to explain to his fellow scouts, but his lips didn't move. He slept and woke, slept and woke, slept and woke. Each time he woke he saw his mother quietly rocking and watching him. He could tell she had been crying, but he didn't know why. In a dazed way he wondered if he had done something wrong.

Dutchie came late in the afternoon to see how Scooter was and brought the news that the game had gone on. Troop 23 had won, 4 - 3. Dutchie told Scooter that he had been hit by a ball that Doolie had thrown, and that after Doolie saw Scooter bleeding and almost dead, he had gone off the field, sat in the grass and cried. Then he went home and didn't play again. "Nobody's ever seen Doolie Higgins cry before."

A short time later, Scooter had forgotten the story. In fact, he didn't even remember that Dutchie had stopped to see him. But even with his mon-

179

strous headache there was one thing Scooter was trying desperately to remember. What had happened to his bat and mitt? When he asked his mother, she said she believed Dutchie had delivered his things when he visited. Then, realizing Scooter did not remember Dutchie's visit, she told him about the game and about Doolie.

When the Fourth of July fireworks went off on Dewey hill that night, there were five to six thousand people lined up on Harbor Avenue and on Main Street. It was a spectacular display, but Scooter didn't hear or see it. He was sound asleep under the watchful eye of his mother in her rocking chair. His sleep would not have been as sound if he knew what his mother now knew—that Dutchie had brought Scooter's bat home, but not the Mel Ott Professional Model Mitt.

When the game was over, Scooter's bat was rounded up by Coach Farley and given to Dutchie to bring to Scooter, but his mitt was not to be found. They all hoped that a family member or a friend of the family had picked it up for safekeeping.

They all were wrong.

* * * * * *

Doctor Higgins came Sunday morning around

ten o'clock as he had promised. He changed the dressing and seemed satisfied with Scooter's progress, especially since he could now remember getting hit. While he still had a headache, it was no longer a pounding one. "I recommend you start sitting up in bed for short periods, and maybe by suppertime you'll be fit enough to go downstairs for a meal," the doctor had said. "Meantime, Mrs. Secory, the wound site shows some signs of infection. So use the ointment generously and if the infection continues, call me."

* * * * * *

"When are we going to tell him we don't know where his mitt is?" Ruth Secory asked the two men sitting across the table from her.

"I don't think we should say anything until he asks. There's no use upsetting him until it's necessary," was Scooter's father's opinion. The others agreed it was good advice.

"What do you suppose happened to the mitt?" Scooter's mother wanted to know.

"Someone saw it lying there and lifted it," was Grandfather Secory's guess.

"But they're all Scouts. I can't believe any one of them would do such a thing."

"Not everyone there was a Scout, and even a Scout or two is not above needing a mitt in these times," Peter Secory observed.

* * * * * *

It was while he was sitting up in bed going through his baseball cards that Scooter got his first visitor. He had heard the doorbell but didn't think much about it until his mother called to him. "Gregory, you have a visitor. Mind you're decent."

When the door opened to his room, it was a girl, a pretty girl in a blue checked gingham dress with a blue gingham ribbon in her hair. No, this wasn't Casey. This was definitely Cassandra.

"Hi Scooter! How ya feeling?"

"Some better. Still got to stay in bed for a while. Still got a headache, but not like yesterday."

"When I saw you lying on the field, I was scared you were dead."

"So was my ma, I guess."

"What did it feel like, getting knocked out, I mean."

"One second I was wondering why the first baseman had his glove fixed to catch my head instead of the ball. The next second I heard a loud crash and ever'thing went black."

"Did you hear you won the game?"

"Dutchie told me. He said that Doolie sat down and cried after."

"Yes, and he went home after that."

"Dutchie told me that, too."

"Actually, nobody felt much like playing after that."

There was an awkward pause in the conversation that Cassandra finally broke.

"Dutchie told me that you thought I was a boy."

Scooter could feel himself blushing. This was the most embarrassing moment of his young life. "I. . . I. . .judged by how good of a ballplayer you were," he stammered. "I never saw any girl who could play good as you. I never thought anything but that you were a boy. I mean, I never saw you in a dress or anything. That's why I told you. . . .." Scooter couldn't bring himself to continue.

"To pee in the bushes like you barbarians do all the time?"

"Yes."

"That's when I figured you didn't know. Everybody else knows from school. You came new, so how would you know? Today I kept my Sunday dress on so's you'd know for sure. My ma's worried I'll go to the Hollow and play ball in it. She warned me good."

"Want to see my baseball cards?"

"Yeh, but I gotta go. My aunt is over with her kids–from my uncle that got killed at the sawmill–and I should be helping. Besides, I'd like to get out of this dress and get some clothes on. I'll see you around?"

"Sure.

"You sorry I'm a girl?"

"I wish the Scouts would allow girls so's you could play on our team."

"That'll be the day. They'll never let girls play baseball with the boys, not in our lifetime. By the way, did they ever find who's got your mitt?"

"Dutchie brought it over with my bat after the game."

"Good, I'm glad they found it. So, then. . .see ya later."

"Thanks for stopping by."

"Even if I'm a girl?"

"Even if."

When the blue gingham dress disappeared through the door of his room, Scooter was somehow glad she was a girl.

* * * * * *

It hurt his head to look under the bed to check

for the bat and mitt, but Scooter checked anyway. They weren't there. "Ma, Pa! Will you please bring up my bat and mitt," caused the older Secorys to look at each other in dismay.

"Time for the moment of truth. Who wants to be the bearer of bad tidings?" the older man asked.

"I guess it's up to me," Scooter's father answered.

"I'll go with you," his wife said.

"I'm not going to sit here alone," the old man said.

Scooter knew something was wrong by the looks on their faces and because they all showed up in his room together. Then he noticed that his father had the bat, but no one had his mitt. That hurt worse than his head, much worse.

* * * * * *

It wasn't long after Cassandra left to become Casey again that Scooter heard the doorbell ring. This time he listened, hoping it was someone bringing his mitt.

It was Grandfather Secory that answered the bell. "Yes, he can see visitors, and I think he could use one right about now." Scooter couldn't hear the visitor's response.

"Yes. He's going to be just fine. Come on in, I'll

show you the way."

Scooter heard two sets of footsteps on the stairs.

"Scooter, there's someone here wants to see you."

It was Doolie Higgins!

"Hi."

"Hi."

"You hurtin' much?"

"Some."

"Didn't mean nothin' by it."

Scooter nodded.

"I mean, I just got up off'n second and threw it to first as hard as I could."

"I believe the 'hard as you could' part."

"But to get you out, not to hurt you."

"I'm not faultin' you. You wanted the triple play."

"I wasn't even think'n that. Just get you out."

"I didn't think anybody could have caught Teddy's liner."

"Mostly luck. Prolly couldn't do it again if I tried."

Doolie looked down at his feet. This was clearly an uncomfortable moment.

"I didn't mean to do it, and I'm sorry I hit you."

"S' okay. Your pa says I'll be fit soon enough."

"That's what he tol' me, too." Doolie looked at the neat rows of baseball cards on the bed. "You got a lotta baseball cards."

"This is only part of 'em. My grandfather's been saving 'em for years."

"Got any Ruths?"

"Pret'-en-near got ever' body but Ruth."

"You don't gotta Ruth?"

"Nope. Red wanted a Lou Gehrig and a Roger Hornsby for his Ruth. I offered a Hack Wilson, a Dizzy Dean, a Mickey Cochran, and a Honus Wagner, but Red backed out. Truth be told I would have given him a couple more of these old Piedmont cards to boot. I got a Sherry Magie, a Cy Young, lots of the older ones."

"I brought you a present."

Scooter looked up expectantly. Maybe Doolie had his mitt. But Doolie reached into his shirt pocket and took out a baseball card.

"It's for you," he said as he held it out to Scooter.

It was a Big League Chewing Gum card of George Herman (Babe) Ruth.

"Thanks," Scooter said, but less than enthusiastically.

"It's yours for keeps. I asked around and Red said you fancied a Ruth and didn't have one."

"Thanks." Again it was said quietly and matter of fact.

"My pa gave me a quarter so's I could take you to Mulder's for a Green River or whatever you want. He said I should come over and kiss and make up for beaning you, but I ain't doin' no kissin'. And I ought to be whuppin' you for calling me Lester."

"I'd druther you beaned me again if it's all the same to you."

"Maybe we could go to Mulder's tomorrow before you have to do deliveries."

"Okay."

"I'll come by later to see of you're up to it."

"Okay."

"You still hurting real bad?"

"Not so bad."

"I thought you'd really like the Babe Ruth."

"I do, really I do," Scooter looked a Doolie. "It's just that somebody took my mitt yesterday. I haven't paid anything on it yet, and it's gone already. A Babe Ruth is nice, but I'd give a hunnerd Ruths to get my mitt back."

"Someone took your new mitt? At the field yesterday? After they had to carry you off like that?"

Scooter nodded and couldn't look up for fear Doolie'd see the tears starting to seep into his eyes.

"Nobody can get away with that. It's one of the best mitts around. A kid couldn't play with it, ever'body'd notice it. I'm real sorry. I'da liked a mitt like that myself."

Who are you and what are you doing in Doolie Higgins' body? Scooter wondered to himself. Maybe the kid from the street and the ballfields was Doolie and this kid in his bedroom was Lester. But he didn't think it wise to ask.

"Thanks for bein' alive," Doolie said quietly.

Scooter looked at Doolie wondering what he meant.

"After the ball hit you, I saw you weren't moving an' bleeding all over the ump's shirt, I was scared I'd killt ya. A Ruth card's nothing to having you not be dead. I'm not sure I coulda' lived with myself if I'd a killt ya. . .." His voice grew quiet. "Don't mind admittin' I was scared."

Doolie stopped talking and looked away. Scooter could see he was having a hard time not to cry. Doolie took a deep breath and continued, "Besides, I got two of that Ruth.

"I gotta go. I hope they catch the kid that stole your mitt. You take care, ya hear. I want another chance to beat the 23 come the championship game. Next time I'll warn ya' when the ball's coming for your head."

"Next time I'll know to duck."

Chapter Thirteen

The Witch Doctor

"Grandfather Secory, would you see if Gregory is feeling up to coming down to supper?" Ruth Secory asked her father-in-law. "Tell him we're having chicken soup and fresh bread. I thought that would go easy on his system."

"It's not the widow Bach's chicken dumpling soup, is it? That stuff'd kill a kid in Scooter's condition."

"No. She offered, but I remembered how you suspect it's what did her first husband in. But she gave me the idea, and I found a recipe in Mother Secory's file."

"Ah," he said nostalgically. "She made good soups. I'll fetch Scooter." And with that, the old man headed for the stairs.

When he came down he said, "He's washing up. I think he's feeling better. He was holding his bat in one hand and the Scout manual in the other learning the Scout Law. Get some of that soup in him and he'll be back playing baseball in no time."

Ruth Secory looked at her father-in-law. "I've

been wondering if all this baseball is good for him. It nearly got him killed, he's all broke up over losing his mitt, and all's he thinks about is baseball."

"Wait until he starts thinking about girls. Then you'll wish he was playing more baseball."

"No, I'm serious. . .." Scooter's mother stopped in mid-sentence as Scooter came down the stairs. "We'll talk later," she whispered.

* * * * * *

Scooter's appetite had returned. Much to his family's relief and amazement, he stowed away two big bowls of soup and three slices of thick white bread with butter and strawberry jam. His headaches were gone, and already his head was starting to itch where he had been hurt, a sign of healing. Dutchie came over after supper and the two boys sat on the front porch and talked. Scooter told of his visit from Doolie. "He's even going to take me to Mulder's for a Green River or a Boston Cooler or whatever I want. His pa gave him the money."

"He must be feeling guilty," Dutchie replied.

"It's a real drag, not being able to play ball for a few days. There's nothing to do but hang around the house. I've got the Scout junk all memorized, and I've tied a hunnerd knots."

"Did your mitt show up yet?"

"Nope. I'm afraid it got swiped. My grandpa called around to the kids in the troop. Nobody's seen it."

"'Sa shame. I can't think a scout would take it."

"Somebody did," Scooter said with finality. A few minutes of silence followed.

Dutchie changed the subject. "Why don't you come meet me at the docks tomorrow morning when we get in and I'll show you the boat. My uncle won't care. He's let me take my friends on before."

"Really? I'd like that. I'd have to ask my ma, but I think I could."

When the mosquitoes got bad, Dutchie went home and Scooter went up to his bedroom.

The adults sat around the kitchen table with a cup of coffee and a plate of cookies. After she heard Scooter's bedroom door close, Ruth Secory returned to the conversation she had started before supper. "I'm not sure it's a good idea that Scooter's so wrapped up in baseball. That's all he thinks about."

"It's something to do in the summer, a harmless pastime," her husband replied.

"Harmless? It nearly got him killed and me scared to death."

"That was an accident. Accidents can happen

walking across the street. We can't protect him from accidents."

"I just don't know that all this baseball is good for kids. Besides, now his heart is broken over the loss of the mitt."

"If I may," Grandfather Secory interjected. "I think these work-up games are good for kids. It helps them learn to get along. Every day they have to decide who bats first, who pitches, who is out and who is safe, who is right and who is wrong. Learning to work these things out amongst themselves is learning to get along, to compromise. I think it's an important part of growing up."

He paused to eat a bite of cookie and sip his coffee. Then he continued. "I think kids' sports, in this case baseball, can be a little slice of life that a kid can experience before the tough job of being a grown-up sets in.

"Here's what I mean. A kid comes to the ballfield with his gear and his experience just like he goes to school every day with the knowledge he has so far. Coaches teach him the game and the rules, just like his parents and teachers educate him. There are rules in baseball just like there are rules in life. There are umpires to enforce the rules in baseball, just like there are policemen and judges to enforce the rules in life.

"And," the old man continued, "how a player uses his skills, what he has learned from his coaches, and his knowledge of the rules of the game determines the outcome of the game. In the same way, how a person uses his ability, his education from school and home, and abides by the rules will determine his success in life. In baseball there is instant reward or punishment. Safe or out. The child understands that. If he can translate that into life, baseball will have been a great learning experience." With that, the old man got up to get another cup of coffee.

"So what do you say about his accident?" Peter Secory wanted to know.

"I say two things. There should be no argument that young Master Higgins learned a life lesson. And I think we can show Scooter learned a lesson or two as well."

"Like?"

"Like, even in a bad misfortune, good can come out of it. In his case, a Babe Ruth baseball card and a Boston Cooler from the town bully. Who knows? They may even become friends and maybe Scooter will be a good influence on him. Then there was a visit from a pretty little girl in a blue gingham dress."

"Father Secory! You are incorrigible!" Ruthie paused. "Scooter's just a boy. He shouldn't be noticing girls for a long time."

"Ruthie, my dear, he'll be in long pants before you know it. He'll get his driver's license at fourteen, and that's only a year and a half away."

"What are we going to do about the mitt?" Scooter's father asked.

"I'd say we report it to the police and wait to see if it turns up."

"We don't know for sure it's stolen. Maybe someone saw it and is keeping it safe for him," Ruth Secory offered.

Both of the men looked at her. The good woman wasn't capable of thinking the worst in people.

She paused to take a sip of her coffee "There is one thing I am worried about. When I last changed his dressing, I think I saw infection in the wound."

* * * * * *

Scooter was still sleeping the next morning when Merrill Secory spotted the widow Bach coming toward the house carrying a plate covered with a red checked cloth. He grabbed the egg basket and headed out the back door. "Morning to you, Mrs.

Bach," he said without giving her a chance to start a conversation.

"Yoo-hoo, Ruthie," she yodeled thorough the screen door.

"Oh, Mrs. Bach. Won't you come in?"

"Oh, thank you. That father-in-law of yours spends enough time with his chickens, don't he? He's almost married to them, if you ask me. I made another batch of sugar cookies. I seen how your older boy and little one liked 'em, so this here's a double batch. Fresh out of the oven, too. How is your boy? Heard tell he got quite a knock on the head. Lottie Witham, lives next door on the other side, her grandson plays on one or 'ta other of those teams. She was there and saw the whole thing. Told me all about it. Scared ever'body half to death, him twitching and bleeding all over the place like that. I bet you were scared to death. What's the doctor say, he gonna be all right?"

"Well. . .."

"I know'd it scared Lottie Witham, I can tell you that. Me, I don't like to see youngsters gettin' hurt. I suppose nobody does. But I've seen enough blood in my day. Did I ever tell about the time my cousin Charlie got his foot crushed by a horse? Shouldn't been foolin' around the barn barefoot, I always say.

But he never did listen to any sense."

Just then Scooter appeared in the kitchen door. His appearance as a living person seemed to startle the widow Bach into a temporary pause.

"Gregory! Sweetie! How are you feeling this morning?" Mrs. Secory was delighted to see her son up and about.

"My head itches where I got hit."

"Itchin's a good sign, if you ask me," the good Widow lost no time in jumping in. "Many's the time I've said, 'if it's itchin' and twitchin', it's getting better.' Took quite a bump on the head, did you? That's what you get for playing those rough games with hard balls and clubs and such, if you ask me. Why can't they use a softer ball, heh? I'd like to know the answer to that."

"Come over here, Scooter. I should change your dressing first thing and get some fresh ointment on your wound." Scooter came over to his mother and turned around so she could get at the dressing. The widow Bach leaned over to see what there was to see and what could be reported to the neighbors as well.

As soon as the dressing came off, Scooter heard Mrs. Bach suck her breath through her teeth and mutter, "Infection. There's infection there or I'm

Granny Goose. What did that sawbones of a doctor give you for that? Never mind, anyone can see it's not working. You stand right there," she said as she got out of her chair all business like. "I'll be right back with a proper poultice. Don't cover it up 'til I get back. Won't take me a minute," and she was out the door.

"What are we gonna' do, Ma? I don't want Granny Goose her putting spider webs or rat poop or nothing like that on my head."

"You stay here, I'm going to get your grandfather in here. And don't you be callin' her Granny Goose. We have to respect our elders." With that she went and called her father-in-law.

Merrill Secory came in smiling. "So you've hired yourself a new doctor, have you Scooter? I heard her sputterin' as she lit out of here. Gone to get her poultice, I suspect. You've gone from modern medicine to a witch doctor. Well, in this case, I've got to give the old biddy her due. The young Boersma lad had an infection in his foot that he doctored for weeks. They thought he might lose his foot. The Widow Bach got wind of it and brought over some of her witch's brew and it cleared right up. Same with Donny's Uncle Brum. Had a nasty gash on his leg. Closed up all festered like and it was the widow

Bach's poultice that got him on his feet in no time.

"There's a lot of speculation what she's got in there, all the way from chicken manure to fish guts. But whatever it is, it works. I think it's mostly fish guts. That's what it smells like."

"Yoo-hoo, I'm back." The old woman was carrying a white porcelain jar. When she took the lid off, Scooter could smell why his grandfather thought it contained fish guts.

"Ma?" Scooter protested.

"Now you just put this on for three hours and if it's not better, I miss my guess. The redness will be gone and so will some of the swelling. It won't be itching so much either. Now slather it on good."

* * * * * *

It took some persuasion, but Scooter's mother let him go down to the docks to meet Dutchie's boat. It was coming through the channel when Scooter arrived at the river, and he watched as Dutchie expertly guided the fishing tug to the dock where his uncle and another man lashed it to cleats with thick ropes. The boat was called *The Don*.

"Did they name it after you?" Scooter shouted over the chug of the diesel engine.

Dutchie grinned and nodded as he killed the engine.

"How you feeling, young man?" Dutchie's uncle called out. "Heard about your noggin gettin' a crack. Did it knock any sense inta your head?"

"I hope so. I think I've learned to duck next time and to take better care of my mitt."

"Hasn't showed up yet?" Dutchie asked.

"Nope."

"Well, c'mon, hop on," Dutchie motioned and Scooter stepped aboard.

"Whew!" Dutchie exclaimed when Scooter got close. "You got fish guts in your pocket?"

Scooter explained about the widow Bach's poultice.

"Well, don't let any seagulls get near your head. They smell that, and you'll have more'n that poultice on your head. My uncle used that stuff on his leg once, didn't you, Uncle Brum?"

"Yep," was the reply. "Worked great when nothing else seemed to. Only thing was a number of seagulls wanted to marry my leg. You better be careful near the lake. Young fella like you might get carried away if enough of them get wind of you," he said with a twinkle in his eye.

Dutchie showed Scooter the pilothouse and the wheel and switches. There were wooden boxes of fish stacked on the rear deck. All the fish were cleaned and arranged in neat rows. "As they pull up the nets, they throw all the fish in those big boxes. Then when we head in, the men clean the fish and put them in clean boxes."

"What to they do with the guts?"

"We sell them to the widow Bach," Dutchie's uncle called out with a laugh.

"Throw 'em to the seagulls," Dutchie said. "Look out the channel. That's the *C. J. Bos* coming in. See all the seagulls around her?"

Scooter could see hundreds of the large screeching birds wheeling and diving around the boat.

"They're eating the guts," Dutchie continued. "We just throw them overboard and the seagulls clean up ever' last bit, sometimes before they hit the water."

As Dutchie talked, a man approached the tug with a newspaper rolled under his arm. He handed the paper to Dutchie's uncle who unrolled it on the deck. Then he opened a locker and took out two fish, placing them on the paper.

"I could use three or four if you got 'em to spare," the man said.

"You got it," Mr. Nagtzaam replied and put another couple of fish in the paper. Then he rolled the paper up and handed it to the man.

"Thank you very much. You have no idea how much this helps," the man said as he tucked the paper under his arm.

"You're very welcome. Glad to do it," the fisherman said, and the man turned and walked away.

"Your uncle gives his fish away free?"

"They were monkeys."

"Looked like fish to me."

"Ha, ha. We call 'em monkeys. They're undersized lake trout that get caught in the nets. They're illegal to catch, but they're deader'n a door nail when we haul 'em in. Uncle Brum doesn't want to waste good fish when so many folks is struggling to put food on the table. So he gives them to poor people who come down. If'n he sold them, he could get in a lot of trouble, but he figures no judge would fine him if he gives the monkeys away to people who are starving."

"They look like bigger fish than the chubs."

"Yeh, they make big holes in the nets, too. The guys'll spend a good couple a hours fixing the nets ever' day."

Just then there was a blast of a loud whistle right behind them! Scooter wheeled around to see a large freighter making its way out of the channel to the lake. It was loaded with cars, dozens of them. Scooter guessed they might be Chryslers.

"Wow! That scared the b'jeebers outa me."

"That's the car ferry. Nearly every day they take a load a' cars like that to Milwaukee. Saves them a trip around the lake." They watched the big steamer make its way down the channel, its big propellers churning up the dirty river water. Then Dutchie said, "C'mon, let's get going. Maybe we can get in on the tail end of work-up before the noon whistle."

"I'm not supposed to play."

"I can. And you can watch, can't you?" And with that they were off to Mulligan's Hollow.

* * * * * *

"You're having company right after lunch," his grandfather said between bites of his liverwurst sandwich that noon. "An old friend of your Grandma's and mine is the eighth grade teacher at Central School. Her name is Nettie Abrams."

"Of course, you'll call her Miss Abrams, won't you, Scooter?" his mother interrupted.

"'Course, Ma."

"Miss Abrams likes to meet new kids, just to get to know a little bit about them before school starts. She's a great lady. I think you'll like her. I read in the paper the other day that she is sponsoring her nephew and his family to come to America from Germany. He was a banker and saw the handwriting in the wall with this Hitler fella. He's lucky he had a relative in the United States to bring him and his family over here. She says there's a boy about your age. Maybe she'll bring him along."

After lunch Mrs. Secory decided to change Scooter's dressing. "I think we ought to check on this infection," she said. "If it's not better, we're going to ring up the doctor."

"My goodness," she exclaimed when the dressing came off.

"Is it worse, Ma?"

"Heavens no! It's a lot better. The redness is gone and the swelling is way down."

"It doesn't itch either. I'd forgotten about it itching."

"That poultice is a wonder," his grandfather acknowledged. "If it didn't smell like rotting fish guts, the old woman could make a fortune selling it."

Scooter's mother had just finished putting a clean dressing on when the front doorbell rang.

"That'll be Nettie. . .er. . .Miss Abrams. Come on, Scooter. Let's meet your new school teacher."

Miss Abrams was a mere wisp of a woman with

very white skin and jet-black hair. She moved with grace and dignity and gave the impression she was very much in control. Her voice was soft and lilting. Scooter found himself being very quiet so he could hear every word she spoke.

A tall, slender boy stood beside her. He was about his own age, Scooter guessed, and he was wearing a funny little cap on the back of his head.

"Scoo... ah, Gregory. I'd like you to meet Miss Abrams. She will be one of your teachers this fall at Central School. Miss Abrams, this is Gregory Secory, my grandson, and his mother, my daughter-in-law, Ruth Secory.

"I'm very pleased to meet you, Gregory," the teacher said as she glided forward to shake Gregory's hand. Her hands were soft, but her grip was firm. "And you as well, Mrs. Secory. And I'd like you to meet Samuel Greenberg, my nephew who just came to this country from Germany. Samuel, this is Gregory. *Samuel, sie sind Gregory Secory und Grossvater Secory.*"

"*Guten Tag, Herr Secory und Gregory. Es freut mich, Sie kennenzulernen,*" the boy said shyly.

"*Danke, Samuel, es freut mich auch. Wie geht's?*" Grandfather Secory replied.

"*Gut, danke.*"

The old man turned to Scooter. "He said 'Good day to you, Master Gregory. I am pleased to meet you.'"

"Doesn't he speak English?" Gregory asked.

Miss Abrams turned to the boy and nodded to him. "Lit-tull bit," the boy said carefully, holding up his hand with his forefinger a little space apart from his thumb.

"He has had some English in his school in Germany," Miss Abrams said quietly. "I think with a little practice and encouragement, he'll get along quite well. I am hoping that the boys in the neighborhood like you and Donald Nagtzaam will include him in your games. Could you do that, Gregory?"

* * * * * *

"Gee willikers, Gramps. I didn't know you could speak German," Scooter exclaimed after Miss Abrams and her nephew had left.

"You knew I came from Germany when I was about your age. My mind's gettin' old and my tongue's slowing down, but I can remember some of it. You don't forget things like 'hello' and 'nice to meet you' and "how about a kiss, young lady' and such," the old man said with a grin.

"What was that funny cap on the kid's head? It

was pinned to his hair."

"It's called a yarmulke. It's worn by a lot of Jewish men and boys. It's a sign that they are observant. That is to say, they are serious about their faith and beliefs."

"So he's Jewish? How come they left Germany? Because of Adler?"

"That's Hitler, Adolf Hitler. Miss Abrams said they were a wealthy family in Berlin. Samuel's father had a very responsible job in the Deutche Bank, but the Nazis falsely accused him of stealing from the government. He lost his job and their money in the bank was frozen. They got out of Germany before they arrested him with just a little more than their clothes and Mrs. Greenberg's jewelry."

"Just like when you were a kid, huh, Grampa?"

"Almost. We had to get out because we were hungry. The Greenberg's had to get out just because they're Jewish."

"Sort of like Satchel Paige can't play baseball in the Major Leagues just because he's a Negro. It's not fair, is it?"

"No, Scooter my boy, it isn't. But like I said before, life isn't fair. And outcomes are determined more by attitudes than circumstances. Mr.

Greenberg didn't let his outcome be determined by the circumstances. He did something about it, just like my parents did.

"And speaking of outcomes and attitudes, here comes Doolie Higgins up the walk. You ready for a Green River with your new friend?"

"You betch 'yer life, but I'm thinking I'll go for a Boston Cooler."

Chapter Fourteen

The Championship Game

Scooter ordered a Boston Cooler and Doolie a Green River.

"You gotta get a Green River, Scooter. They beat a Cooler any ol' day."

"Okay, make mine a Green River, too."

"You won't be sorry."

Scooter wasn't, the cold tart syrup 'hit the spot' as his Grandfather would say.

Doolie had a few pennies left over so he bought two sour apple candy sticks, which they sucked on as they walked home.

"Did you hear we got new kid in the neighborhood," Scooter asked.

"I heard he's a Hebe."

"What's a Hebe?

"You know, a Hebrew. He's Jewish."

"He's Jewish all right. He wears a funny little cap with a funny name. He's Miss Abram's nephew. She came over and asked me to play with him."

"Does he play baseball?"

"I dunno. I'll call for him in the morning, and

we'll see once."

"Why not now?"

"Can't. Gotta do deliveries."

"I got paper routes. The *Herald* in the mornin'
and the *Trib* in the afternoon."

"Two routes? Gee, how many customers?"

"I got twenty-nine *Heralds* and forty *Tribs*."

"How much do you make on two routes?

"Exactly three dollars and twenty-five cents a
week. How much do you make doing deliveries?"

"Dollar a week. Sometimes I get tips. I'm earning money to pay back my pa for my mitt."

"Did your mitt show up anywheres yet?"

"No. Someone's got it, and I'm thinking if'n it
hasn't showed up by now, it ain't gonna."

"Stole?"

Scooter just nodded.

Doolie thought to change the subject. "How
much money do you get in tips?"

"Sometimes I get a nickel. But you always got
to watch out for biting dogs. And sometimes bigger
kids try to beat you up."

"Why'd they want to do that?"

"Like if'n you called 'em names. You know, like
Lester."

At the sound of the word Lester, Doolie stopped

walking.

"You know I ought to whack you for that."

Scooter stopped and turned to face Doolie. "You won't though, will you." Scooter said it as a statement, quietly, like Miss Abrams might have said it.

"Oh, won't I? Why won't I?"

"'Cause you don't want to see me dead. You said so yourself yesterday."

With that Scooter put his stick back in his mouth and turned and started walking—although he was ready to run. Then he heard Doolie laugh.

"Scooter, you're something," and ran to catch up.

"Thanks, and thanks for the Green River."

"You're welcome. You take care of yourself, ya hear? I don't want your dying on my conscience. And somethin' else, have you got a dead fish in your pocket?"

* * * * * *

The next morning Scooter took his bat and ball and went over to Miss Abram's house to call for Samuel. It was Miss Abrams that came to the door. "Why good morning, Gregory. Just a minute, I'll get Samuel."

"Want to play baseball with us?" Scooter asked

when Samuel came to the door.

Samuel looked at Scooter with a puzzled look and then turned to Miss Abrams.

"*Werden sie baseball spielen?*" she asked him.

"*Ya.*"

"Good, come on. The game'll be starting soon." Scooter led the way to the Hollow. Six kids were already on the field, but they had no bat. Ah, Scooter thought, the power in a bat. "This is Sammy Greenberg. His family's just come over from Germany. He's Miss Abrams' nephew. He needs to make friends, so I brought him. We'll let him be all-time catcher."

They all nodded.

"Ibbidy, bibbidy for first-ups?" he asked.

"Sure."

"Caller gets pitch?"

"First base!"

"Pitch!"

"Okay."

"Good, put em' up." And they all got in a circle around Scooter and held their clenched fists out. "Ibbidy, bibbidy, sibidy, sab, ibbidy, bibbidy, k'nahbull. Ibbidy..."

The rules were called and agreed to; pitcher's hands is out, automatic second, force at the plate, and hitters getters.

Then Scooter said something he hadn't needed to say for a few weeks, "Dibs on bats and mitts." They all nodded.

All of this must be very confusing to someone who doesn't speak English, thought Scooter as he watched Sammy take in the proceedings. What he didn't realize was that the majority of the English-speaking world would have no idea what had been decided either.

Casey and Red were up first, Scooter as the caller was the pitcher, and the rest took their positions in the field. Scooter motioned to Sammy to stand behind the plate.

"You," Scooter said as he pointed to Sammy's chest, "Watch." Scooter got behind the plate. "Pitch me a ball, somebody," and he demonstrated the duties of the catcher.

He pointed to Sammy to get behind the plate. "You–catcher," he said to Sammy and turned to the pitcher. "Throw a pitch to him."

Sammy didn't catch the ball but scrambled after it and turned to throw it back to the pitcher. He brought the ball over his head as Scooter had done and flung his arm forward. In the process he failed to bend his elbow and released the ball too late, flinging it straight into the ground. There were some snickers behind some mitts.

Scooter took Sammy's hand and sat him in the grass by home plate. "You," he said pointing to Sammy, "watch." He shaded his eyes as if he were looking at the field.

"*Ja, Ich vahtch.*"

"Yah, you watch. Learn baseball."

"*Vahtch bazabahl.*"

"Yah, watch baseball."

It was Casey who, after a while, suggested they give Sammy a chance to bat.

"Okay." Scooter agreed. "Sammy, come here," he said and motioned the boy to come to the plate. He held the bat out to Sammy and pointed to it. "Bat."

"*Ist ein Schlagstock.*"

"Ah, you know it. We call it a bat."

"Baht."

"Right. Bat."

Scooter moved him so he was standing ready to bat. "Pitch him one, Woody."

Sammy swung the bat at the pitch without bending his elbows just like someone might swing a rope with a heavy object on the end.

"No, Sammy. . .watch," Scooter said as he did a demonstration swing. "Like this. See?" Then he turned to Woody. "Move in a little closer, Woody. Let him hit it."

Despite another awkward swing, Sammy did manage to hit the ball, a slow roller to Woody. As he has seen the others do, Sammy ran toward first base. "Out," called Woody as he picked up the ball. It meant nothing to Sammy. When he reached first base he just kept running the bases at top speed. Woody threw the ball to Red who ran and touched Sammy with the ball before he got to second base. "Out," called Red. But that out made no more sense to Sammy than the first one had. He kept right on running.

It set them all to giggling, and by the time Sammy triumphantly stepped on home plate, they were howling.

"We gotta teach him the rules, Scooter," Woody said thoughtfully, "before he can play."

* * * * * *

"I play bazabahl," Sammy said as they walked home after the noon whistle.

"Yes, you played baseball," Scooter said slowly, taking care to enunciate carefully.

"I run fest, ja?" Sammy said and marched his first two fingers across his other palm.

The Championship Game

"Yes, you ran fast."

"Vas means 'ibbidy, bibbidy'?" Sammy asked. "Ist English?"

That stopped Scooter dead in his tracks. He couldn't keep from laughing, and for a second, he forgot about the missing mitt.

* * * * * *

The next few weeks passed quickly. The effects of the concussion lasted only few days and the wound healed rapidly, thanks to widow Bach's magic poultice.

Scooter passed the requirements to become a Tenderfoot Class Scout. That meant he could finally wear his scout uniform and the Tenderfoot badge. The troop held a formal installation ceremony and Gregory Peter Secory became an official member. He immediately began working on the requirements for Second Class Scout because, as he told his grandfather, "Tenderfoot sounds too much like a rookie."

Sammy became a regular in the work-up games. His baseball and his English improved rapidly. Scooter's grandfather taught Scooter some German words, and with Scooter's new-found German and Sammy's improving English, the two boys managed

216

to communicate.

Scooter did so well at his delivery job that old man Cashmere gave him an apple nearly every other day. He had already paid $2.85 on his debt for the Mel Ott Professional Model Mitt, the mitt someone else had under their bed. The thought of it made Scooter so mad he threw an apple at a tree he was passing. It exploded into countless pieces, but it failed to make Scooter feel better.

The Saturday after the Fourth Troop 23 beat the Lutheran troop, 7 - 5. The next week they beat St. Pats, 8 - 4. The only team they played that wasn't a Scout troop was one sponsored by the American Legion. In the past a few of the Legion players had been accused of unsportsmanlike behavior, such as calling the Scouts sissies. They also made fun of the Scouts' pledge by yelling, "Have you helped your old lady across the street?" or "Have you cranked the car of a one-armed man today?"

Before the game with the American Legion team, Scoutmaster McHenry insisted on exemplary behavior and urged his Scouts to "talk back with your bats." They did just that. Troop 23 scored five runs in the first inning, four more in the second, and mercied them in four innings. The win qualified them to play for the league championship during the Coast Guard Fete. Their opponents would be Troop 24, Doolie Higgins' troop. It was a rematch of the Fourth of July game, Scooter tingled with excitement just thinking about it. He just wished he had his mitt.

* * * * * *

"C'mon, Woodrow. Swing that bat like you mean it," Coach Farley urged. It was Troop 23's Thursday practice before the championship game. "You used to be a better hitter. What happened?"

"The bat's too heavy for me, Mr. Farley."

"Then get a lighter one. Use the other bat."

"This is the lightest we got. I use ta have my own bat, but Doolie Higgins broke it."

"Then choke up on that one a bit more."

"If I do that the little end hits my stomach when I swing."

"Well, do the best you can, then. Everybody has to pull their weight if we're going to beat Troop 24," Coach Farley said with resignation in his voice. He turned to Scoutmaster McHenry. "I wonder how else the Higgins boy can hurt us. Woodrow's bat, young Secory's head—what's he going to do to us on Saturday?"

"He's a fine ballplayer, but he's only one person," the Scoutmaster observed. "We're every bit as good a team as they. I really think we could win on Saturday. Do you have a strategy, Farley?"

"I'm thinking of starting Gary Slatski as our first pitcher. He's a bit more overpowering than Tommy Hammond. They'll undoubtedly start with Higgins, so I'm thinking power against power. Then throw Hammond against Denton. If Hammond falters, we'll use young Secory. We'll go with the same batting order we've used in the past several games."

"Sounds good to me. Let's announce it to the boys."

* * * * * *

"Pa, could you please make another bat?" Scooter asked when he got home from the practice that night.

"What's wrong with the one I made you? Did you crack it already."

"No," Scooter replied. "It's too heavy for Woody. He used to be a good hitter 'til Doolie broke his bat over a fence post. My bat's too heavy for him. He's kinda little and skinny, ya know."

"No doubt he isn't eating properly, poor thing," his mother observed.

"I don't know of any seasoned ash around. Down at the dock there's some hard maple they use for the racks to dry the nets on. Think hard maple would work for a bat, Pa?" Scooter's father asked the old man.

"I don't see why not. It's for a kid's bat. Should last for a time, at least until he grows enough to use Scooter's bat."

"I'll see." Scooter's father turned to him. "I can't promise. Depends on finding proper wood stock. I'll see what I can do. Should be a little lighter than yours and a bit shorter?"

"And a thinner handle. He's got little hands."

* * * * * *

Doolie showed up for work-up the next morning along with Bub Denton and a kid named Jerry Banning that everybody called Spider. As usual Woody was an easy out, and Sammy made some base running mistakes. But to everyone's surprise, Doolie played fair. He even did hitters getters on a foul ball that he hit into old man Kibben's backyard.

"Who is that new kid? The one who looks exactly like Doolie Higgins, only nice," Casey asked.

Scooter laughed at Casey's joke. "Doolie's okay.

I wouldn't call him Lester though," he cautioned.

"Bub Denton told me that at the last Troop 24 practice, Doolie told ever'body that if he found out who stole your mitt, he'd lay a whuppin' on 'em they wouldn't forget."

"Gee willikers. I guess a bully ain't so bad if he's for you instead of against you."

* * * * * *

Doolie caught up to Scooter and Sammy as they walked home after the noon whistle. "You ready for the game tomorrow?" he asked.

"Doolie, I was born ready. 'Cept I wish I had my mitt."

"You can borrow mine when we're battin'."

"That'd be swell. Casey told me you were threatening to whup anybody on your team if you caught 'em having stole the mitt."

"Figure it had to be somebody on your team or mine. Ever'body says no Scout would steal a mitt, but we were about the only kids there that day, 'cept fer like Casey and Dutchie."

"I'd be grateful to get it back. I haven't even paid my grandpa back for it yet. But any which way, I can't wait for the game tomorrow."

"Should be a good game. You guys find anyone

to replace Woody, yet? What about the Hebe? Is he playing for you guys? He's not bad for a Jew boy."

"If you mean Sammy here, he's not a Scout. And be careful, his English is better than you think."

"I didn't say nothin' bad. I didn't think that Jews played baseball, that's all."

"Ever hear of Hank Greenberg, first baseman for the Detroit Tigers?"

"Geez. I never thought of it. Greenberg's a Jew? What's next?"

"Negroes in Major League baseball."

"That will never happen."

* * * * * *

Peter Secory came home from the fishery that afternoon with a bat under his arm. "When I told Mr. Dornbos what I wanted the maple for, he sent me over to Baker's Lumber. They had some seasoned ash. So here you go young man. A present for Woodrow from Mr. Dornbos."

"Mr. Dornbos certainly has been good to us," Scooter's mother observed. "You're so lucky to work for him."

Grandfather Secory nodded his head. Lawrence Dornbos's not one to forget a favor, the old lender thought to himself.

The Championship Game

Scooter took the bat from his father and rubbed his hands over the smooth wood. It was lighter than his. The handle was smaller, but the end was big. WOODY had been burned in as a trademark.

"Jeepers, Pa. He ought to be able to break his slump with this."

"He slumps? It's probably because he is ashamed that you're hiding him," his mother observed.

Scooter just rolled his eyes. Explaining that would be like trying to explain Ibbidy Bibbidy to Sammy Greenberg.

* * * * * *

It was a horrible night for Scooter. He couldn't get to sleep. The harder he tried, the worse it got.

As he lay awake Scooter's thoughts drifted back to Century Avenue and the work-up games he had played with his old friends. They seemed so far away now. He wondered if his new Jewish friend would have been accepted there—a place where the sound of your last name was more important than who you were. It struck him that in Grand Harbor everybody knew everybody else by their first name. How your last name sounded didn't seem to matter much. Scooter turned to find a more comfortable position.

The Championship Game

Tomorrow was the Coast Guard Fete. There would be a big picnic at Mulligan's Hollow, life-saving contests and demonstrations by the Coasties, a parade down Main Street, and fireworks on Dewey Hill. But to Scooter the main event was the game against Doolie and Troop 24. He wondered if Woody would like the new bat his father had made. He wondered if he would ever see his Mel Ott Professional Model Mitt again. He turned his pillow again and pounded a place to put his head.

By the time Scooter did fall asleep, he was awakened by the widow Bach's rooster. Dawn was just breaking and there was no getting back to sleep. When he finally heard his grandfather's padded slippers on the stairs, he slipped out of bed and followed him.

"My, my! When's the last time you got up with the chickens? Can't sleep, m'boy?"

"Thinking about the baseball game. Championship game, ya know. I don't think I slept but a wink."

"The jitter's 'll do that to ya. How about fetching the paper for a old man whose bones are creaking?"

"Scooter! What are you doing up at this hour?" It was his mother who got up early on Saturdays to get the baking done.

The Championship Game

"Couldn't sleep."

"Ah, sweetie. Thinking about your game, are you? What time do you have to be at the field?"

"Game's at ten a'clock."

"Be here before you know it," she said as she busied herself making bread and blueberry pies. Scooter went to the front porch to get the *Herald* for his grandfather.

Because he was looking for the paper, Scooter didn't see it at first. It was laying upside down, and so when he did see it, he didn't recognize it. But suddenly he understood. Lying on the front porch was his Mel Ott Professional Model baseball mitt. Scooter was so excited he raced back in the house without picking up the paper.

"Well, I'll be jiggered. Someone had a touch of conscience and just threw it up on the porch last night, eh?" his grandfather exclaimed.

"More likely it's because Doolie Higgins sort of offered a reward."

"Doolie Higgins put up a reward if they returned your mitt? What a nice boy. What did he offer?" Scooter's mother wanted to know.

"He offered to lay a whuppin on the kid who swiped it if he caught him."

Merrill Secory couldn't help but chortle, but

225

The Championship Game

Scooter's mother failed to see the humor in the situation.

"I don't approve of all this violence, but I'm so happy you have your mitt back," she said.

"Just in time for the game," Scooter said as he pounded his fist into the pocket of the mitt.

* * * * * *

Woody was already at the field when Scooter arrived. He was swinging one of the team's bats, as if swinging it often enough would make it lighter.

"Hey, Woody, whatcha doin'?"

"I'm swingin' a bat. What does it look like I'm doin'?" There was bitterness in his voice.

"Try swinging this one."

"You got a new bat? Is it smaller? Lemme try it," he said as he came over to Scooter.

"Jeepers, this'n just my size," he said as he waggled it. "Handle's perfect too. Where'd you. . .." he stopped short as he read his name on the bat.

"My pa made it for you. To help you outta your slump'."

"Gee willikers, Scoot. Your pa made it just for me? Thanks a lot."

"Naw, he made it for me. He just put your name on it and made it smaller for fun'un. 'Course it's for

226

you!"

Just then Slats arrived. "You found your mitt? Where was it?"

"Showed up on our front porch during the night."

"Wow, and just in time for the game. And you got a new bat, Woody?"

"Scooter's pa made it for me. Pitch me some, Slats. I'd like to get the feel of her before the game."

* * * * * *

As game time approached, there was so much excitement the air almost crackled. Scooter felt as if his stomach was crackling. Every other player had butterflies or knots in their stomach as well. There were blankets on the rise covered with mothers and brothers and sisters. Scouts from the other troops had come to see who would be champions. Scooter spotted Dutchie, Casey, Beans, and Sammy Greenberg in his skullcap. There were some Coast Guardsmen in their dress whites. Scooter's mother was sitting on a blanket with little Russell. Grandfather stood with some other men. Scooter's father wasn't there. Like most other father's Peter Secory worked every Saturday morning, and this Saturday was no exception.

Troop 24 had their flags and colors along the

third base bench as they were the home team. Scooter's Troop 23 had their flags and colors along the visitor's side.

"Gather 'round, 23," Scoutmaster McHenry called out. He stood ramrod straight, his pencil-thin moustache hardly moving as he addressed his troop. "I expect every Scout to do his duty. Your duty is to do your best. There is pride and honor riding on this game. We've all prepared ourselves, and I trust that preparation will hold us in good stead. But win or lose, I'm proud of your accomplishments on the sporting field, and I'm sure your parents are as well. Now, here's Coach Farley who has a few words of instruction for you."

Coach Farley took a step forward to address them. "Well, gentlemen, this is it—the championship game. The way we started out this season, I didn't think we would ever make it. But here we are. We'll throw Gary Slatski in there pitching the first three innings and see if we can't get a lead and then hold 'em.

"I think I know how excited you all are. It's important to settle down and get your head in the game if we are to win. I hope you all do your best so that you can look back on this game with fond memories. Now, let's play the best baseball of our lives and bury those guys!"

The boys cheered and shortly after similar sounds came from the other team. Scooter was sure their coach had given them much the same pep talk.

"Play ball!" the home plate umpire called out. Scooter recognized him as the same umpire who had called the bases in the Fourth of July game. Doolie led his team onto the field and went to the pitcher's mound. Scooter saw Spider Banning was playing third, Bub Denton short, and Packy Witham second. A tall kid they called Hex and whose name was Bobby Kleinhecksel played first base.

Tommy Hammond led off the inning for Troop 23. Doolie shouted "lefty" when he saw Hammy coming to bat, and he didn't pitch the ball until Spider, following Doolie's direction, moved more toward the third base foul line.

"They're not giving Hammy the line this time," Slats whispered.

"Doolie knows better," Scooter replied. "I got a feeling it ain't gonna be easy today."

Slats nodded in agreement.

Scooter knew that even Doolie was feeling the jitters, because he walked Hammy on five pitches. "Way to watch 'em, Hammy," Slats shouted as Hammy trotted to first.

The Championship Game

"Benjamin Stone, you're up," Coach Farley said, as if Stony didn't know it. "Look 'em over good. He's got some wild ones in him this morning."

If Doolie did have wild pitches in him, he didn't show any to Stony who was out on three straight pitches. "Looks like he's just trying to throw strikes, Slats. Get in there and camp on one of 'em," Scooter urged.

Slats did just that and with the chorus of "aay, batta, batta" from the fielders he lined Doolie's first pitch to center field. Hammy scooted around to third when the ball bounced off the heel of the centerfielder's mitt and got away from him momentarily. But Slats was held on first.

Cries of "c'moan, Scooter, knock 'em both in," and "you can do it," and "take 'em to the fence, keyed" greeted Scooter as he walked up to bat.

"You all healed up, kid?" the umpire asked.

"Hope so," Scooter replied and took his position—feet about shoulder width apart. He reached out and tapped the center of the plate with the bat in his right hand and began taking slow nonchalant practice swings. He stared at Doolie who was grinning. The war of looks began.

Pitch it over the plate if you dare, or are you gonna walk me?

The Championship Game

You can't hit my pitching if your life depended on it.

Oh no? Bring it over, let's see.

Scooter knew Doolie would try to get the first pitch over the plate, so he made up his mind to go after it. But it was inside, and Scooter didn't get much of his bat on the ball. He sent a grounder between Spider and Bub, the shortstop. Spider charged the ball, but it took a bad hop and passed him. Bub Denton had to go a long way to his right, but he fielded it cleanly. By that time Hammy was almost home, and there was no chance to get Slats out at second. The only play he had was to get Scooter out at first. It was a close play and Scooter thought he hit the bag before he heard the ball hit Hex's glove. But "out at first" was the umpire's call.

Teddy VanderVeen popped up to Doolie and 23's half of the inning was over.

In Troop 24's half of the first inning, with two men on base, Doolie hit a fly ball that the left fielder misjudged. Both men on base scored and Doolie wound up on third base. The inning ended with Slats striking out two batters in a row. Scooter's Troop 23 was behind 2-1.

Chapter Fifteen

The Strangest Play
in Baseball History

There was no scoring in the second inning. Both teams stranded runners on base, so the score remained 2-1 in favor of Doolie's troop.

Woody was the first batter in the third inning. He stood in the batter's box with such confidence he looked like a different kid–almost dangerous. But not to Doolie. He threw Woody an "easy out" look before delivering his first pitch.

Woody did not go down easily, and after fouling off several pitches managed to draw a walk. He tossed his bat down and took off for first base, but not before sticking out his tongue at Doolie. "It ain't over yet, Woodrow, I'll get you," Doolie muttered.

Hammy was next up. "Lefty," Doolie called to his players. "Not you, Spider. Don't give him the line."

Hammy took a mighty cut at Doolie's pitch. Spider took a step or two back away from the batter. Scooter was just about to whisper to Slats that

it was a perfect time to bunt toward third when
Hammy did exactly that. It was a slow roller that
danced and twisted down the line but stayed in fair
territory. Neither Doolie nor Spider had a chance
to throw Hammy out, and Woody advanced to second.

Troop 23 had two on and nobody out with Stony
coming up to bat. Doolie took off his cap and wiped
his forehead with his sleeve. Stony dug his feet into
the sand of the batter's box to get a good foothold.

Stony worked Doolie to a three balls and two
strike count before Stony hit a sharp grounder to
Spider who raced over to step on third to force
Woody out. He then threw the ball to first base,
but the throw was wide. The ball got past Hex and
the runners advanced to third and second. Troop
23 now had runners on second and third with only
one out and Slats at the plate.

Slats hit Doolie's first pitch again, this time lift-
ing a high fly ball to center field. The center fielder
drifted back and caught it, but the ball was hit so
deep it allowed Hammy to score from third base
and Stony to advance to third. Troop 23 now had a
runner on third with two out, one run in and Scooter
coming to bat.

The visual conversation between Doolie and

Scooter began as soon as Scooter got himself set and faced the pitcher.

You won't get your bat on this one.

You don't dare put one down the center.

The first pitch was high and outside for a ball.

I can't get my bat on it if you're too scared to put it where I can reach it.

I ain't scared of anything. See if you can get your bat around on this one.

The pitch was right down the middle, and Scooter watched it right into the fat part of his swinging bat. The ball rocketed back at Doolie with such speed that Doolie had all he could do to put his mitt up to protect his face. The ball thwacked the heel of his mitt and caromed toward the first base line. Since Doolie's vision had been blocked by his mitt, he didn't know where the ball bounded. When he turned and saw it, he raced after it. But the ball was well into foul territory before Doolie reached it. Scooter was safe at first and Stony had scored.

When the screaming and yelling died down, Troop 23 saw Doolie walking toward the umpire. "It's a foul ball," he protested. "I picked it up in foul territory."

The home base umpire came out toward Doolie.

"Sorry, you first touched it on the mound. That makes it a fair ball, no matter where it goes after that."

Doolie reluctantly made his way back to the mound, rubbing his forehead.

"You okay, Lester?" Scooter called, grinning at the pitcher.

"Yeah. You nearly killt me. What'd I ever do to you, Gregory?" he responded with a smile.

"Even Steven?"

"Even Steven."

And with that Doolie struck out Teddy VanderVeen with three straight pitches.

* * * * * *

When Troop 24 came up to bat in the bottom of the third inning, Slats threw only three pitches. The first batter popped out to the catcher. The next batter hit the first pitch on a line drive straight at Red, who caught it easily. The last batter hit a pop-up to the infield that any one of them could have caught, but Slats waved off and caught it himself. At the end of three innings Troop 23 led 3-2.

"C'mon, you guys. We need some more runs. Let's get some hits—just put the ball in play. Let's go," Coach Farley urged. "Looks like we're facing the Denton boy. We've hit him before. We can do it again. C'mon now! Red, you're up first. Start us off with a hit."

Red did just that—a clean single up the middle. Chappy moved him along to second with a great bunt that Bub Denton couldn't field in time. Suddenly there were runners on first and second with no one out. Mike Beck then fouled several pitches off, including a long fly ball that cleared the left field fence. At that, Doolie called, "Time!" and walked to the mound. They both looked over to the visitor's side of the field to see that Woody was the next batter. After a few words were exchanged, Doolie returned to his place at shortstop.

Bub threw two pitches way outside and Becker got a walk, loading the bases. This brought Woody to the plate, the same Woody who was in a hitting slump. But this same Woody had a new bat—a bat that had already been named by Slats as "the Woody Special."

"Throw strikes," Doolie called to Bub. "This guy can't get it out of the infield."

Woody dug into the batter's box and pounded the plate with the Woody Special. Bub took Doolie's advice and concentrated on throwing a strike. It turned out to be bad advice as Woody drilled the first pitch over Doolie's head into left center field. Both Red and Chappy scored easily, and Beck stopped at second. Woody fairly danced a jig of happiness on first base. He had just knocked in runs number four and five, and Troop 23's lead was now 5 to 2 with runners on first and second with nobody out. If Woody could have caught Doolie's attention, he would have stuck his tongue out at him again.

But the team's good luck ended. Hammy grounded to the second baseman to force out Woody. Stony popped up to the catcher, and Slats hit another fly ball to the left fielder who caught it and ended the inning.

Troop 24 went three up and three down in the bottom of the fourth, and Scooter's team loaded the bases in the top half of the fifth inning, but couldn't push anyone across the plate.

In the bottom half of the fifth inning, Doolie's team began to rally. Their first batter bunted and Hammy fell as he tried to stop the ball. He threw the ball to first while sitting on the ground, but too late. The second batter popped out to Slats in foul territory. Hex was up next and hit a sharp grounder into center field between Hammy and Chappy, the second baseman. The runner on first moved all the way to third on the play. Bub Denton singled, scoring one run and sending Hex to third. Spider Banning came to bat and hit a grounder to Scooter who threw the ball to Chappy at second, forcing Bub for the second out.

Hex had hesitated before trying to score, taking off for home when he saw Scooter flip the ball to Chappy. Chappy fired the ball to home after stepping on second base, but it was too late. Hex slid in safely and in the process upset Teddy. Before the young catcher could collect himself Spider had raced to second.

"Time out!" called Coach Farley, and he made his way to the pitcher's mound. All the infielders joined him.

"How you feeling, Tommy?"

"Good. Nobody's tagging me good. They're all just grounders. We just gotta get one more out."

"Right. The score is 5 - 4 in our favor with two outs and a runner on second. What do any of you know about the next batter?"

"Packy Witham. Plays work-up with us lots."

"How good is he?"

"Good as the next kid. He can hit, but not as good as Doolie."

"Okay. I'd like you to pitch carefully to the

Witham boy. Don't give him anything to hit. If you walk him, we'll have a force out at any base."

"Isn't Doolie up after this next batter?" asked Scooter. They all knew the dilemma. Should Tommy walk Packy and pitch to Doolie with two runners on base, or should he try to get Packy out and let Doolie lead off the next inning with no one on base?

"Nothing says you have to give Higgins anything to hit either. A walk to him doesn't hurt us, and we still will have a play at any base," Coach Farley answered.

"I ain't scared of Doolie," Hammy said with a sneer. "I say we walk Packy and pitch to Doolie. We'll have a play at any base."

"I like your attitude, Tommy," Coach Farley said. "We're only four outs away from winning this thing, fellas. Let's all bear down and win it," he said and trotted back to the bench.

Hammy pitched carefully to Packy and walked him. That put runners on first and second with two out and Doolie Higgins at the plate.

Scooter was anxious. He knew Doolie was loving the situation. He could tie the game or even put his team ahead with one swing of the bat. Scooter could read the look on Doolie's face as if it were a neon sign. *Bring it over Hammy. I double dare you to give me something I can hit.*

Hammy's first pitch was high, but Doolie was so anxious to get a hit he went for it and fouled it straight back to the backstop. The next pitch slipped wildly off Hammy's fingers and got past Teddy and the runners each advanced a base.

Suddenly the situation had changed. Instead of having a play at any base, the only play they had was to get Doolie out at first.

"C'moan key-ed, humithard, nothing good nouw-ah," Scooter chatted to Hammy, all the while pounding his mitt while the rest of the players sang the "aay batta, batta" song.

Coach Farley had signaled the outfielders to move back when Doolie came to bat, but even so, when Scooter saw Doolie connect with Hammy's next pitch, his heart sank. It was a high line drive that was headed between Stony in center and Woody in right. Stony raced back and to his left, while Woody ran back and to his right. Meanwhile, Scooter raced to the outfield to get the relay, hoping they could hold Doolie to a triple.

What happened next was relived by Scooter every time he met Stoney as they grew up and grew old. *Stony leaping in the air and catching the ball. Stony bobbling the ball momentarily as he was fall-*

ing. Stony reaching out with both hands to cradle the tumbling ball into his mitt as he crashed into the grass.

"Unbelievable catch, Benjamin!" yelled Coach Farley as the boys trotted to the bench and a tumultuous welcome.

Scoutmaster McHenry was the only one remaining calm. "There's another inning to play before the contest is decided. We mustn't let our exuberance get in the way of our concentration. One run is not a comfortable lead."

The first half of the sixth and Troop 23's last chance to bat went quickly. Chappy led off and hit a line drive that Doolie speared. Becker flew out to the left fielder, and Woody lined the ball hard, but right at Bub Denton.

As they took the field, Troop 23 had "Only three more outs, lads. Only three more outs and victory is ours," ringing in their ears.

The inning started out badly with Hammy walking the first batter and the second hitter drilling a ground ball between Red and Scooter. Red missed it completely, and Scooter was able to get his mitt on the ball, but could only knock it down. That put runners on first base and second with nobody out. The next batter struck out. The following batter

241

was a skinny kid named Clarence that everybody on the Troop 24 team called Tad. An easy out, Scooter thought, as he watched Tad hold his bat with his left arm pointed straight back so his fore-arms formed a straight line. But Hammy hit Tad with an inside pitch to load the bases.

"Where's the play 23?" Coach Farley shouted.

"Force at the plate!" was the answer.

"Right. The play's at the plate!" the coach reit-erated the instructions. Then suddenly he had sec-ond thoughts. "Time out!" he called and trotted to the mound.

The base umpire moved toward the mound as well. There would be no stalling at his ball game, and this was Coach Farley's second visit to the mound in two innings. "Let's move this along, coach," he warned.

"Yes sir!" Coach Farley replied to the umpire. Then he turned to his players. "Okay, fellas. There's two out. The play is at the plate, but if you are sure of it, a double play will win the game for us. Their catcher is up to bat. Don't everybody look at him now, but he's a bit overweight, and I noticed he doesn't run well. So you might think about going for the double play if you have it. Okay? Let's go."

What happened next was the strangest play anyone at that game had ever seen. The runner on first was the skinny kid called Tad. The fat kid at bat was a left-handed hitter, so all the fielders shifted a bit toward the right side of the field. The batter chopped at Hammy's first pitch and sent a sharp ground ball toward Chappy, the second baseman. As Chappy moved to his left to field the ball, Scooter moved toward second base, certain that Chappy would throw the ball to him for the double play.

But at that moment the ball hit Tad as he was running from first to second, and before it got to Chappy! It bounced off Tad with enough speed to carom well onto the grass in right center field. Both Scooter and Chappy raced after it. Scooter got there first and picked it up in time to see that the runner who had been on second had already rounded third and was streaking for home. He represented the winning run!

Scooter threw the ball to home with everything he could muster. There were shrieking cheers and shouts of "Run!" and "Slide!" as well as desperation cries of "Home it!" and "Tag him, Teddy".

The cries mingled with the clouds of rising stone dust as the ball and the runner each tried to beat the other to the plate. Teddy caught the throw and tagged the runner as he slid across the plate. For an agonizing second the outcome of the game hung on the judgment of the umpire, who hesitated for a moment, then flung his arms out from his sides and screamed, "He's safe."

Troop 24 broke into pandemonium and raced to hug their player who had scored.

Chappy slammed his mitt to the ground in disgust. Scooter's legs lost their will to hold him up, and he plopped down on the outfield grass watching Doolie and the others from the team throw their caps and mitts into the air.

Scooter looked down at the grass. It was too much to watch. His team had led almost the whole game, and now they had lost it because of a freaky play.

Stony had trotted in from his position in center and was about to plop down beside Scooter when he stopped and said, "What going on? Scooter, sumpin's going on. Look!"

Scooter looked up to see Coach Farley and Scoutmaster McHenry engaged in a serious conversation with the umpire at home plate. Coach Farley was pointing at Chappy and saying "interference." The base umpire was running toward the three of them with his hands in the air calling "Time out!" as if to stop any violence that might break out.

The Strangest Play in Baseball History

Scooter got to his feet, looked at Chappy and Stony, and shrugged his shoulders. The meeting had expanded to include Troop 24's Scoutmaster and coach. Troop 24's bench had quieted too, sensing something was wrong.

The home base umpire sent the coaches to their benches as he and the base umpire moved toward the pitcher's mound. Scooter knew the umpire's conference was serious when they each got out rule books and began thumbing through them, mumbling passages to each other. Finally the umpires signaled the coaches to the meeting.

After a few words from the home plate umpire, Coach Farley and Scoutmaster McHenry started smiling and nodding in apparent agreement with the umpires' decision. Troop 24's Scoutmaster and coach shook their heads. "Show me that in the rule book," one of them demanded. The home plate umpire handed him a rulebook with his thumb on one of the lines.

"The game is over," the umpire announced in a loud voice. "The visiting team is declared the winner by the score of 5 to 4."

Shouts, mitts, and caps went flying in the air—this time different voices, different mitts, different caps. Scooter fairly danced to the bench. There were

245

back slaps and handshakes and hugs. Now it was Troop 24's turn to slam their mitts to the ground and sit down in disgust.

"What happened, Mister Farley. How come we won?" Woody asked.

"Gather 'round, team," Scoutmaster McHenry called for order. When everyone had calmed down he continued. "There is an important lesson to be learned here, Scouts. It is that to play the game successfully, it's important to know the rules. Coach Farley here saved the day for us because he knew the rules and how they should be properly applied. I don't take anything away from your accomplishments on the field, but we owe Coach Farley a debt of gratitude and I'll let him explain."

"As you may recall, boys, they had the bases loaded with one out. The rules state that if a batted ball hits a base runner before the batted ball passes a fielder, that runner is out, the ball is dead, and there can be no further play. So the runner who got hit with the ball was out, and the first run didn't count because the ball was dead.

"However, the rules go on to state that if there was a chance that the batted ball could have been turned into a double play, two outs are declared—the runner who gets hit by the ball and the runner who is closest to home plate. Because there could have been a double play, two are out on the play so the game is over. And the base umpire heard us talking about possibly going for the double play when we were talking on the mound, so that cinched it for us.

"You all played a great game and you deserve the championship. Slatski, great pitching; Benjamin, outstanding catch; Woodrow, you came out of your slump just in time to knock in the winning run for us; I'm so pleased for you, Woody. Everybody played great: Scooter, Red, Tommy. Now, Scoutmaster McHenry promised me that if we won, he would treat us to ice cream at Mulder's. Let's hear it for him. Hip hip. . ."

"Hurray!" was the loud response.

"Hip, hip. . ."

The next "hurray" was even louder.

* * * * * *

Parents and friends started coming off the rise to mingle with the players. Dutchie was all smiles and was as happy as if his Troop had won. Casey came down, too, and gave Scooter a full-on hug and a kiss on the cheek. "Great game!" she said. Scooter was momentarily embarrassed, but then Casey hugged Slats and Woody, too.

Sammy was next to shake his hand, "Wery goot bazebahl game, yah? You team are za best! Ve say in Shurmun: *prima, ausgezeichnet!*"

"Thanks, I think. That "out-of-sight-net"–is that a word or did you just sneeze?" Scooter asked with a grin. He turned away from Sammy to look for his family and ran smack into Doolie and his father.

"I see you got your glove back. Who had it?"

"Showed up on the front porch during the night. Probably someone was afraid of getting a whuppin'," Scooter said with a grin. "You know, like if'n their pa caught 'em with it, or something," he quickly added.

Doolie smiled back. "Yeh, or something. Anyway, nice game, Gregory. If we'd a had one more inning, we'd a beat ya," Doolie said as he held out his hand.

"Not bad yourself, Lester," Scooter replied as he shook it. "And if it hadn't of been for that catch Stony made on you, maybe you would have.

"If 'ifs' an 'ands' were pots and pans, beggars would ride horses," Doctor Higgins said. "Congratulations on a fine game, son. You played like you're fully recovered."

"Thank you. I think I am, sir."

"Good. Come Lester, let's go home and get some

248

lunch. I'll bet you're starved."

"See you around, Lester." Scooter said

"Later, Gregory!" Doolie said smiling as he and his father turned to go.

Grandfather Secory had found his way down to the field and scooped Scooter up into a big hug. "I'll bet they didn't have a championship game on Century Avenue this morning!" he said.

That just about told the whole story in one sentence, Scooter thought as he looked up at his Grandfather. Suddenly he felt himself fighting tears.

"Thank you, Gramps," he said softly. "You really can pull peppermints out of the air, can't you."

"There's only peppermints to be found where there really are peppermints. This peppermint was always here–just waiting for you to find it."